Bodie

Lawyer Josh Thorn believes in the law and justice. Even so, when he agrees to defend prostitute Rosa May Whitefield, he knows he jeopardizes his standing in the community. In 1880 the mining town of Bodie, California, averaged a killing a day, but Rosa May's crime broke all the rules when she killed one man and wounded two others because they beat and raped her.

Powerful forces line up against Josh and the girl, and her fate appears sealed until two killers arrive looking for Josh. With the help of friends, Josh orchestrates a jail break. A vigilante posse tracks the fugitives into the High Sierras before events lead Josh back to Bodie for a final showdown.

© James Hitt 2018
First published in Great Britain 2018

ISBN 978-0-7198-2778-5

The Crowood Press
The Stable Block
Crowood Lane
Ramsbury
Marlborough
Wiltshire SN8 2HR

www.bhwesterns.com

Robert Hale is an imprint
of The Crowood Press

The right of James Hitt to be identified as
author of this work has been asserted by him
in accordance with the Copyright, Designs and
Patents Act 1988

Typeset by
Derek Doyle & Associates, Shaw Heath
Printed and bound in Great Britain by
4Bind Ltd, Stevenage, SG1 2XT

Bodie

James Hitt

A Black Horse Western

ROBERT HALE

PART I

ROSA MAY

'Virtue Lane harbors no white roses, only soiled flowers.'

—quoted in *The Weekly Bodie Standard,*
April 1, 1880

1

Using his sleeve, Gunderson Lott wiped the beer from his blond mustache and studied his cards. For the first time that night, he held a decent hand: three jacks. Already he had lost well over a hundred dollars, but he could make up some of his losses with one good pot.

Jud Ash, a burly miner, sat on Gunderson's right, and he opened the betting with a silver dollar. Rather than raise, Gunderson controlled his temptation and called. The betting circled the table, and all seven men stayed. This was good because it meant a bigger pot.

The door opened, and Rosa May entered, carrying a tray of beers. They all knew the whores employed by P.T. Cain, the man who sat on Gunderson's immediate left. They were playing cards in Cain's establishment, the Emporium, and Rosa May was his top girl. She projected an innocence and freshness that belied her profession. Every man in the room watched her, unable to remove his eyes.

Gunderson had never spent an evening with her, although he felt the stirring between his legs. Hell, what need had he of a whore when he could have any woman in town without paying a wooden nickel?

Once she laid the drinks before the men, she withdrew to a dark corner where she waited for the game to break up.

Whenever Cain played poker, he liked to have her near because he believed she brought him luck. Since he had hired her over a year before, his business had tripled, and no saloon/bordello in town did better than his.

Gunderson left his beer untouched because he was already a little drunk. They were all drunk, except Cain and Dave Hayes, neither of whom ever drank at all. Gunderson threw in one card, a deuce, and held on to a ten. It was a stupid ploy, and he knew it. He should have thrown away the ten, too, and drawn two cards, but he had played smart all night, and it had gotten him nowhere. Now he hoped the others would know that he was drawing for a straight or flush.

Smith, who dealt, tossed a card to him, and Gunderson slipped it in with his others, not daring to look at it. Slowly with his thumb and forefinger, he exposed each card until he reached the one he had drawn. Another ten. A full house, jacks over tens. By God! The pot was his for sure.

Play it smart, he told himself. Stay calm. Don't react. Don't let them know what you've got. Sucker them in.

Ash opened with a two dollar bet. Gunderson called. Cain raised five dollars.

Up to that point, the night belonged to Cain. He had a stack of gold coins before him that amounted to over $600. Jud Ash called, but Smith raised another five.

Dave Hayes threw in his cards. Ben Lauter, the deputy marshal, stared at his cards so long that Cain said, 'Make up your mind, Lauter. We don't have the whole night.'

Lauter fingered his money before he tossed his cards on the pile. Lauter had no guts. He never did when he played cards.

The bet returned to Gunderson. Only four men remained in the hand, and he knew it was time to make his move.

'I call—' He tossed in a ten dollar gold piece, '—and raise ten more.'

He tried to remain calm, but his heart beat furiously.

Cain curled his lips into a smile. 'Well, well. Gun hit.'

Gunderson hated to be called 'Gun' the way Cain said it. His father called him 'Gun' in exactly that tone, and it made him feel like a child.

Cain ran his fingers along the edge of his cards, flicking them. 'Guess I'll have to pay to see what you've got. But let's make it interesting.' He tossed in two twenty-dollar gold coins. 'Raise thirty.'

With a disgusted grunt, Smith threw in his cards. 'Too rich for my pockets.'

Ash glared at his cards before he tossed them in the pile. 'I'm out,' he said.

Gunderson would have raised again, but he had only enough to cover the bet plus another five or six loose coins in his pockets. Still, the pot had swelled well beyond his losses for the night. His luck had definitely changed. With a flick of his wrist, he threw in his last coins.

'Call,' he said.

Cain spread his cards on the table. Four queens stared up at Gunderson, their stern, unsmiling faces lacking all traces of sympathy.

'Damn!' he said, and threw his cards into the pile.

Cain raked in the money.

'Had 'em to start.' Cain smiled broadly. 'You should pay attention to the draw, Gun.'

As much as he hated people calling him 'Gun,' he hated even more people giving him advice when he hadn't asked for it, and Cain was always giving him advice. Cain knew such tactics irritated Gunderson, and he appeared to enjoy the younger man's discomfort.

Gunderson swept up his glass and gulped the beer in one swallow. 'A hundred on the cuff,' he said to Cain.

Dave Hayes who sat quietly most of the night, winning

8

about as much as he lost, stood and slipped his coins in his pants pocket.

'Enough for me,' he said to Gunderson, 'Time to go home, son. You've had enough for tonight. We all have.'

'Yeah, me, too.' Lauter slapped on his Stetson, and together with Dave Hayes, left the room.

The others scooped their coins from the table, all except Cain, who stacked the folding money and twenty-dollar gold pieces into two neat piles. He said, 'The game is over for tonight, Gun. Next week. That is, if you get an advance from your daddy. No more on the cuff.'

The little bastard was refusing to advance him any more money. Gunderson owed him less than $500 all told, which was nothing, a piss in the pot as far as the Lott family was concerned. Cain's actions showed a total lack of respect, a total disregard of Gunderson's position within the community. The mines kept Cain in business, and Gunderson's father was the principal shareholder of the Bodie Mine. Last year alone, the mines dug more than five million out of the mountain.

And here Cain refused him a lousy hundred dollars on the cuff. Well, if Gunderson wasn't going to leave the table a winner, he was going to leave with something, even if it were nothing more than a roll in the sheets.

'I want the whore.' With his thumb, he pointed to the girl who sat in the corner.

Cain slipped one stack of coins off the table and stuffed them in his pockets. He didn't bother to look up at Gunderson. 'Rosa May's not feeling well tonight. Bit of ague, I suspect.'

'I said I wanted her.'

This was how you handled men like Cain. You let them know who was in charge.

From the doorway, Dave Hayes said, 'You're drunk, boy.

Go home.'

To Smith and Ash, Gunderson said, 'Come on, wouldn't you like a little extra to tap off the evening?'

Jud Ash rose to his feet, his massive body casting Rosa May deeper into the shadows. 'She sure is pretty.'

Gunderson pushed his chair back and crossed the floor to the girl. Without a word, the laconic, Smith followed, his expression passive and cool. Behind them Cain laughed nervously.

'Gentlemen,' he said. 'Gentlemen, please.'

Rosa May came to her feet. Gunderson reached for her, his hand dropping from her shoulder to her breast.

'Come to Uncle Gunderson,' he said and laughed.

With a snarl, she raked his cheek, her nails drawing blood, and he screamed in surprise. With a flick of his wrist, he threw a backhand that sent her crashing against the wall.

Cain jumped to his feet. 'Don't hurt her!'

With sudden fury, Gunderson grabbed the front of her dress and jerked with such force that the cloth ripped from her shoulders, exposing the top of her chemise. He pulled her forward, and she slapped him, her hand stinging his cheek. He struck her again, this time a wide swinging open hand blow. She hit the floor, her eyes staring at the ceiling but unfocused. Gunderson, Ash and Smith towered over her.

'Don't hurt her.' Cain tried to push through the group, and Smith slammed an elbow into his chest that sent him gasping for air.

The girl raised her head and stared into the faces of the men. For the first time, fear pinched her eyes, and this excited Gunderson.

He began to unbutton his pants. 'Uncle Gunderson has something for you.'

By the time they had finished and sent her away,

Gunderson and Smith had roughed her up a bit more. Both had given her a taste of knuckles when she had struggled.

Still wheezing from the blow, Cain, sat in a far corner, his head turned away so that he didn't have to witness what they did to his favorite whore. Gunderson ordered the little saloon keeper to bring them another bottle of his best rye. Cain pushed himself from the chair and shuffled out of the room.

Gunderson called after him, 'Tell the whore that Uncle Gunderson thought she was a real good little girl.'

They were laughing when she appeared out of the black hallway, the top of her dress hanging in tatters around her shoulders. Gunderson never noticed people's eyes, but he noticed hers. They were like glass, dead and distant. He was still staring into those eyes when she raised the sawed-off shotgun.

Twin explosions rocked the small room.

Gunderson was on the floor. Although he had never closed his eyes, he could not remember how he had gotten there. He heard a man moan and tried to raise his head to see who it was, but his muscles refused to obey. Then he realized it was he who was moaning, and with that realization, pain engulfed his chest and face, pain so intense, so completely overwhelming he could only close his eyes and scream for it to go away.

2

Josh held his glass of claret aloft in a salute to his host who sat at the dining table across from him.

'As usual, another wonderful meal, Mrs Lott.'

He enjoyed his twice weekly dinners with the Lotts. This particular evening was no exception. As usual, his belly ached from too much beef and beans.

Ruth Lott acknowledged the compliment with a slight tilt of her head. She was a stern little woman who tied her gray-streaked hair into a tight bun. Her appearance mirrored her politics. She was always making a fuss about the wickedness of Bodie, especially the Chinese of King Street and the women of Virtue Lane. As one of the founders and pillars of the Law and Decency League, she believed her destiny lay in eradicating sin in Bodie, a foolish task if not an impossible one. The very first time Josh met her, she had leaned close and whispered to him as if they were co-conspirators, 'Bodie is Sodom, Mr Thorn, and the Lord is going to strike this town dead. Mark my words. Strike it dead.'

Susan smiled and laid a hand on Josh's. She wore her blonde hair piled on her head and held in place by combs. Stays and ribs constricted her already trim waist, and once or twice during the evening he had caught a glimpse of her high-laced boots, polished until a bright sheen covered every inch of the leather. Of course, Susan had not polished the boots. That job fell to the maid. However, the care Susan took with her attire reflected the care she took with every aspect of her life.

Word had already spread around Bodie that the prettiest girl in town was engaged to the smartest lawyer in town, although if the truth be known, Josh had yet to ask her. He was sure he was in love with her. How could any sane man not be? Until now, he avoided the commitment. Exactly why, he was not sure.

As usual, Gunderson, the Lotts' son, failed to dine with them. Since this was Saturday night, he was at the Emporium, playing poker and carousing to all hours of the night. His reputation with the ladies hinted that he played too rough. Rumors circulated that he had compromised a half-dozen young ladies of Bodie. Neither of these facts failed to dissuade others from casting their nets for him. After all, a marriage with Gunderson would be a union with one of the largest fortunes in the state.

Thomas Lott removed a pair of cigars from his vest pocket, offering one to Josh.

'Perhaps the ladies will excuse us for a while?' His chest strained against his vest, threatening to separate the buttons from the cloth. His big, raw hands, the hands of a man who had worked the placer mines, were clutched into knotty fists.

Susan slipped her arm through Josh's. 'Not tonight, Father. Josh and I are going to sit on the porch for a while, and I do not want him smelling of that ugly weed. It is a beautiful night out. Really it is. So clear.'

'And cold, my dear,' said Mrs Lott. 'There is still snow on the ground.'

'Only patches, Mother. We will wear our coats.'

Smiling, Thomas Lott slid the cigars back into his pocket. 'All right, my dear. However, I do need a few minutes with

Joshua. Five minutes is all I ask. Ten at most.'

'Ten. No more than ten minutes,' said Susan.

'On my honor.' Thomas Lott crossed his heart to seal his promise.

Lott led Josh into the library where he dropped into a comfortable chair. He poured Josh another glass of claret. Josh understood immediately this was to be a continuation of the conversation from the previous week.

'You have thought about it, my boy?' asked Lott.

'Little else, to be frank.' Josh sipped the dessert wine, a little strong, but he enjoyed the aftertaste. 'If I come to work for you, I must give up my regular practice. I hesitate only because so many depend upon me.'

'The Chinese, you mean. Your reputation was made defending them, but you waste your talents on rabble. Frankly, my boy, it is time for you to move forward. A new circle of friends could prove quite rewarding.'

'If I turn my back on the Chinese, who will defend them? You know as well as I that the other lawyers in this town refuse to have anything to do with them.'

Lott gulped his wine and wiped his mustache with the palm of his hand. Mrs Lott had expended much effort to make a gentleman of her husband, but Lott's habits from the old days persisted, especially when he was in the company of other men.

'They can find someone else. Import a struggling lawyer from Frisco. You really must sever all ties with this Sammy Chung. Some big fees would certainly have come your way except for your acquaintance with that fellow. And, too, you have gotten about as much use out of the man as possible.'

'When I was down and broke, Sammy gave me the chance to get back on my feet,' said Josh. 'Without him, I would not be in this living room having this conversation.'

'That man is behind every crooked deal in this town. I

believe he is even behind this union unrest.' Lott pointed an accusing finger at Josh. 'Unions are foreign nonsense, imported by atheists and agnostics. Like this Marx fellow. Have your read his book?' Josh shook his head, and Lott said, 'An unreadable piece of trash. Nevertheless, a dangerous philosophy in the wrong hands. America is a country for business, and men like this Sammy Chung and his crowd come over here and want to change things. By God, I will close the mine before I allow a union in. I tell you, Joshua, we must send these people back from where they came.

'The Chinese were brought to build the railroads. Most had no choice. At any rate, none of the owners allow the Chinese to work the mines. You allow them to do your laundry and to carry loads of lumber into town. You allow them to do all sorts of menial work, but not in the mines. I seriously doubt Sammy has much influence with the miners.'

Laying his wine glass aside, Josh told himself to calm down, to control his temper. Otherwise he and Lott would soon be yelling at one another, and that would get him kicked out of the house. He certainly had no wish for that, not again.

He said, 'Look, Mr Lott, I will make a deal with you. I will see if Sammy Chung has any connection with this talk of unions. If he has, which I doubt, I will come to work for you and you alone. However, if he has no part in it, I cannot give him up. His people need someone, and for the moment, that someone is me.'

Lott removed one of the cigars from his vest, bit off an end, and spit the remnant in his hand. He stuffed the discarded piece in a vest pocket. 'I am offering you quite a lucrative position, my boy. Are your yellow friends worth such loyalty?'

Josh said, 'If I turn my back on Sammy Chung, how can

you be sure I will not do the same to you?'

The old man struck a Lucifer on the bottom of his boot and lit the cigar. A cloud of smoke soon engulfed his head and shoulders. Lott peered at Josh through half-closed lids.

Josh had seen that look only once when he come to the house to discuss the rights of a placer miner whom the Bodie Mine claimed was digging on their property. When Lott got that look in his eyes, Josh had little trouble believing the old man was as ruthless as his reputation.

Waving his hand in front of his face to clear the smoke, Lott said, 'Son—' He always called Josh 'son' when he was about to make a pronouncement, '—good judgment is just as valuable as loyalty. Without it, you may give loyalty to the wrong person. Surely you understand that?'

'I will pray for guidance, sir.'

Lott gave a nod. Like his wife, Lott was a Sunday-morning-go-to-meeting Methodist, convinced of God's power to move mountains and provide a large and steady income for those who deserved it. If Josh would pray, God would show him the way.

'The Bible is our guidepost.' Lott puffed on his cigar. 'All the answers are there.'

Susan entered the room, her forehead rolled into a wave of unbecoming wrinkles. 'Well, Joshua, at least you refused to indulge in that nasty old weed. I smelled it all the way in the back of the house. And now, Papa, you have far exceeded your ten minutes. Come, Joshua. Let us go sit on the porch. It is a beautiful night.' She held out her hand.

Smiling, Lott took the cigar from between his teeth and waved it like a wand. 'You are right, my dear. Go enjoy the night, whatever it may offer.'

Josh and Susan settled themselves on the porch in two stiff-backed chairs and watched the stars sparkle in the clear, cool night.

'Now tell me,' she said. 'Tell me all about San Francisco. Is there anything new in the dress shops? Are the fashions changing?'

Josh laughed. 'I know nothing of fashions, Susan. I went there on business, which had nothing to do with dresses and bonnets. I spent most of my time with stuffy merchants settling old accounts. At any rate, what does it matter? Whatever is in San Francisco arrives here in a matter of months, and you have it.'

She hugged herself, pulling her coat tighter across her bosom. When she spoke, her breath showed against the light from the front window. 'Do you think, after we are married, we can live there? It would be so exciting.'

'I am not rich, you know,' Josh said.

'But you will be. Papa says so.'

He wanted to lean over and kiss her, but behind the front window the shadow of her mother loomed. He remained rooted to his chair. The situation made him feel a bit like a naughty child about to be scolded.

Later, when the Lotts wandered off to bed, Susan took him inside where they removed their coats, and half-chilled, sat in front of the blazing fireplace. The divan was large and comfortable, and they huddled shoulder to shoulder, feeling the additional warmth of each other's body. At last they heard her father snoring and Mrs Lott creep out of their bedroom and into the guest bedroom. Only then did they feel safe enough to kiss, a long lingering kiss with open mouths. Susan turned her body into his, and his passion rose so fiercely that he thought the buttons of his pants would burst. She moaned softly, her mouth opening wider, allowing his tongue to touch hers before quickly withdrawing. His hand slipped down her sloping breast until his fingers touched her hard nipple. As always, she grabbed his wrist and refused to allow him to go any further.

Breathing heavily, he sat back. He knew she was right. They should wait until they were married. They stared at each other, the firelight dancing shadows across their faces.

Footsteps approached on the gravel path leading to the porch. A heavy fist pounded the door. Susan jumped to her feet and began to straighten her clothes while Josh went to answer the knock. Throwing open the door, he discovered Marshal Grey bundled in his coat. Grey was in his late thirties, but his blond hair which hung to his shoulders made him appear five years younger. He sported a full mustache that drooped over both sides of his mouth.

Josh stepped aside to allow Marshal Grey to enter. He glanced at Josh and then Susan. Josh had heard rumors that, before Josh arrived in Bodie, Grey had shown interest in Susan. Certainly, the look on the marshal's face appeared to confirm the rumors. In Susan's presence, his expression became almost tender.

Behind him Josh heard Lott descend the stairs. Dressed in a robe, the old man stood beside Josh and laid a hand on his shoulder. Grey took notice, and his expression returned to its stoic hardness.

Lott glanced at the grandfather clock that stood in the entryway. Both hands rested on XI. 'Surely this is not the place you should be at this hour of the night, Marshal.'

'Gunderson has been hurt,' Grey said. 'Doctor Fitzgerald is working on him now. I am sorry. I never wished to come here under these circumstances.' He spun on his heels and went back through the door, closing it behind him.

'My God!' Lott whispered. 'I must get dressed.'

'Should we wake Mrs Lott?' Josh asked.

'No,' Lott said. 'There is no good in that.'

Lott dressed in a matter of minutes, and coming back down the stairs, barreled past Josh and Susan. He had forgotten his coat. He threw open the door and set a brisk pace, which, because rheumatism had settled in his swollen knees, was more shuffle than run. Josh helped Susan with her coat. The thin, night air had grown crisp, and the wind bit into their exposed faces and hands.

Josh hugged his heavy coat to his body. He wished he were still holding Susan instead, and then he cursed himself for a callous villain. Her brother lay hurt, possibly dying for all they knew, and here he was thinking of her body.

His hand fondled the Bible in his coat pocket, and he understood that he would have to pray for forgiveness.

They caught up with the old man as he entered the doctor's house. A blast of heat greeted them. The marshal was there before them, and when they came through the door, his eyes locked on Susan. He held his hat in his hands, curling the brim.

The door to the back room was closed, and a hand-painted sign read *Stay out*. Lott stared at the door as if it hid secrets he was afraid to discover.

'How did it happen?' Susan's voice had become less the little girl and more like a man's, deeper and full of authority.

'One of P.T. Cain's women.' Grey continued to play with the brim of his Stetson. 'He was in a roomful of men playing cards. She came in with a shotgun and opened up. I know nothing more.'

'How bad is he?' Lott asked.

'We must wait and see,' said Grey.

Susan put her arm around her father. Leaning in, she kissed him on the cheek and whispered soft words. He nodded without comment.

When Josh looked at Grey, he discovered the marshal glaring at him with undisguised anger. At that moment, he understood that Susan had lied to him. Early in their courtship, she had told him that her involvement with Grey was nothing more than a mere flirtation. He saw now that Grey was in love with her. Josh was surprised that he had taken so long to see it.

For almost an hour they remained in strained silence, interrupted only by an occasional rustle of Susan's dress as she continued to comfort her father. At last the door opened, and Doctor Fitzgerald emerged, wiping bloody hands on a soiled apron. He was in his mid fifties, the only doctor available for the camp.

'How is my son?' Lott asked.

The doctor met the question with an expression devoid of emotion. 'The left side of his face and left shoulder sustained the bulk of the trauma. The muscles are torn up, and there is bone damage.'

'His face?' Mr Lott said.

'The buckshot tore up one side. There will be scarring.'

'My poor Adonis.' Mr Lott spoke so softly the words barely rose above a whisper.

'When can we see Gunderson?' asked Susan.

'Go in now, if you wish, but understand he is in the arms of Morpheus.'

Susan led her father past the doctor and into the back room. Josh remained behind. This was a private time for Mr Lott and Susan. Josh was still an outsider. He said, 'You appear tired, Doctor.'

Fitzgerald nodded. 'A bit. Yes.'

'If not, I would wonder if you have any feelings for your patients,' said Josh.

Without changing his expression, Doctor Fitzgerald said, 'I have plenty of feelings for my patients, those who are deserving.' Addressing Marshal Grey, he said, 'Smith is dead.'

'It is murder then,' said Grey.

'He did not die of ague fever.'

20

'What of Ash?' asked Grey.

'A couple of buckshot in the right hand.' Doctor Fitzgerald looked at one of the straight-back wooden chairs as if it were an invitation. He dropped into it, slouching. 'Yes, I am tired. I dug shot out of Gunderson for the past two hours.' He closed his eyes and rubbed them with his palms. When he opened them again, they appeared redder than before.

Josh considered taking out the Bible and reading a bit. Instead he leaned back in his chair and waited. During the past year he had found himself reading the Good Book less and less, a problem he must remedy.

At last Susan brought her father back into the waiting room. She walked directly to Grey.

'What will happen to the woman who did this?' She glanced at her father who stood hunched over as if he were in physical pain.

'You must not worry about what is to come. We have the th—' Grey caught himself before he said the word. '—the woman in jail. Justice will be served.' As if to emphasize his words, he stuffed his hat on his head.

Outside, a blast of frigid wind slammed into the building.

After Josh walked Susan and her father home, he returned to his lodgings, leaning into the wind to keep himself upright. Clouds of dust and old snow blew past with frightening speed. While he had experienced a few strong winds since his arrival in Bodie, this was the worst yet. All around him wooden buildings rattled and shook as if trying to escape their foundations.

A light shone through the drawn curtains of the window of his office. Many times when he returned late at night, he found his office occupied, always by the same person, Sammy Chung.

The wind pushed the door inward, and Josh leaned into

it to close it. As he expected, there beside the window sat
Sammy. Sammy was taller than the average Chinaman,
perhaps five seven or eight, and his features were less round
and more angular, which suggested mixed parentage. As
always, he wore a full-length embroidered robe, which Josh
figured cost plenty.

On the table beside Sammy sat a whiskey bottle and two
empty glasses. Sammy poured a finger of whiskey in each
glass. Picking them up, he offered one to Josh.

'Please. Have this with me. It will fortify your courage.'

Smiling, Josh took the glass. 'And why do I need to fortify
my courage?'

'For the favor I am about to ask.' Sammy held the glass in
a salute, and in one quick gulp, downed the whiskey.

'Who do you want me to defend this time?' Josh asked.
'Another cousin?'

Sammy patted his mouth with the back of his hand. 'Ah,
no, my friend. Nothing as simple as that. This is far more
complicated and far more of an imposition. If I had any
other choice, I would not ask such a favor.'

Josh went cold inside. 'The woman. The one who shot
Gunderson and the others.'

Sammy poured himself another drink.

'If I were to represent this girl, I would be risking everything,' Josh said.

'There is no one else who will defend her. I will make a
deal with you. Tomorrow morning, go see the girl. If, then,
you still refuse to defend her, I will understand. Things will
be as they have always been between us. I will ask no more of
you on her behalf.'

'Why do you ask at all, Sammy?'

'After my daughter—' He paused, as if searching for the
proper words. 'After Mai Lin's ordeal, this woman came and
took care of her.' He was referring to a case in which a white

storekeeper had molested the girl. 'I feared for Mai Lin before Miss Whitefield saw to her. The woman was her savior.'

'Smith just died,' said Josh.

'Ah, this is I did not know,' said Sammy.

'Murder is a hanging offense,' said Josh.

'And would this town hang a woman?'

'She opened up with a shotgun on a roomful of men.'

'I cannot deny what she did,' said Sammy. 'But defense is built around reasons, motives, is it not? If anyone should understand why this woman did what she did, it is you, Joshua.'

'What the hell does that mean?' asked Josh.

Sammy stood. 'Go see her, my friend. She will be expecting you. And please, try to reserve judgment. You may be surprised.'

'You told her I would be coming? That was damn presumptuous of you, Sammy.'

'I told her I would be sending someone. She has no idea it is you.'

'If I go see her, how the hell can I explain that to the Lotts?'

'Look at it this way, my friend. For you it may cause a few awkward moments. For Miss Whitefield, her life is at stake.'

Sammy had done it to him again, just like that very first time when he had defended Sing Tong. Sammy always presented his arguments with enough information to whet Josh's interest, and invariably Josh took the case, winning far more than he lost. He had yet to refuse the man, which made Josh wonder what it was in himself that made him so susceptible to Sammy Chung.

As if he divined Josh's thoughts, Sammy said, 'I only came here to ask. However, I have more than hope on my side. I know the kind of man you are, Joshua Thorn. A good man, a fair man. You will listen to her story and make up your own mind.'

Josh held up the whiskey so the light shone through the amber liquid.

'Damn you, Sammy.'

He threw the whiskey down his throat. It burned all the way to his stomach.

3

Unable to sleep, Josh lay staring at the dark ceiling. Outside his window, the gusting wind howled, punctuated by discordant piano chords that drifted north from the saloons. Twice during the night, pistols barked along Main Street, a nightly occurrence to which Josh paid little attention. By four o'clock in the morning, still wide awake, he had come to the conclusion that, under no circumstances, would he defend Rosa May Whitefield. If he did, he would destroy his position in the town and with the Lotts.

He owed the poor girl the courtesy of a visit, if for no other reason than to explain his reasons for refusing to defend her. Whether or not she understood mattered little. He would make his apologies and extricate himself. He could not risk everything to defend a whore who had killed a man, even a man like Smith, a known ruffian and brawler.

Yet, as much as he tried to convince himself that he had made the right decision, the girl's face haunted his restlessness. He had heard all the stories. She was the most desired whore in Bodie, and just about every miner in town, once he had dust in his poke, came to Cain's for a few minutes with her. She gave them what they wanted, and she never cheated them or pinched their pokes. As satisfied customers, they returned again and again. Cain was getting rich off her, and she, if she were like other whores, spent most of her money on nice clothes or whiskey or opium or all three.

For the moment, the miners praised her beauty, but all too soon, like most of those who worked her profession, her beauty would desert her. How long could she retain that innocent face when, night after night, dirty miners sweated and strained against her frail flesh? When her looks faded, she would be left penniless with only bitter memories as companions.

But even that future was lost to her now. Within the month, Rosa May Whitefield would be dangling from the hoist suspended from Bodie's Livery and Feed. There was little anyone could do about it.

Before first light, Josh rose from bed and dressed. Outside, the Bodie zephyr howled as it had all through the night. As he trudged up Main Street, the wind drove sand and grit into his exposed face. He ate breakfast at Mother Mapes, a shack behind the saloons that an old black woman had converted into a kitchen. Without exception, the food was the best in town, and miners crowded the small room from the moment it opened until the first whistle called them to work. There was no menu, only standard fare: eggs, steak, biscuits and gravy.

Josh sat alone in a corner and tried to find solace in his decision. Yet he felt empty, as if a personal tragedy had overtaken him. He withdrew the Bible and allowed it to fall open by itself. His finger found the passage *And the king loved Esther above all the women, and she obtained grace and favor in his sight more than all the virgins.*

He laughed to himself. Men are such fools, he thought. Including me.

Josh slipped the Bible back into his coat. When he looked up, he found Mother Mapes, all five feet of her, standing before him. She had a surprisingly slim waist, but her hips flared to the width of her shoulders. She was well-liked by the miners who flocked to her café for her amiable personality as well as the food.

'That little girl is all alone over there.' Mother Mapes wiped her dark hands across her apron.

'Pardon?' said Josh.

'Rosa May. She got no one. She gonna need someone. You gonna be that someone, Mr Thorn?'

Josh brought the coffee to his lips, trying to hide behind the wisps of steam that rose from the surface.

'Have you ever been to Virtue Lane, Mr Thorn?' Answering her own question, Mother Mapes said, 'No, course you ain't. Those shacks is flimsy little things that bake you in the summer and freeze you in the winter. Not a one fit for a dog, but those women work there. You may not like what they do, Mr Thorn, but they deserve better than that. Anybody deserves better than that.'

Josh lowered the cup. 'Who have you been talking to, Mother?'

'You just go see her.' Mother Mapes shuffled away, and Josh discovered that the room had grown quiet. The eyes of every man in the room were on him.

Rising from the table, he followed Mother Mapes into the kitchen where the odor of sizzling bacon permeated the room. Mother Mapes cooked everything in bacon grease. He cornered her by the stove where she swept up eggs, three at a time, cracking them so that the whites and yokes dropped into a large skillet. She tossed the shells in an open coffee pot. Within seconds a dozen eggs filled the skillet.

Josh asked, 'What do you owe Sammy Chung?'

She glared at him out of the corner of her eye. 'You think Sammy put me up to this?'

'You owe him, Mother?'

'He loaned me the money to buy this place.' She stirred

the eggs so fast and hard that pieces flew from the skillet. 'Because the color of my skin ain't white, no one else in town would give Mother Mapes a chance. Sure, I owe Sammy Chung. Plenty people owe Sammy.'

'I see,' he said.

Once again Sammy Chung, the grand manipulator, was pulling strings behind the scenes, getting Josh to do his bidding. Well, this time, Sammy was going to be disappointed. Josh would be damned before he would help out the little whore.

Mother Mapes stopped stirring and faced him. 'I speak for Rosa May because I want to speak for her. Me. Mother Mapes. Rosa May was a good girl once. She still a good girl. Life made her what she is.'

'She killed a man.'

Mother Mapes raised the spoon caked with half-cooked eggs and waved it in his face. 'You gonna be her judge now?'

Josh took Mother Mapes by the hand and lowered the spoon. 'I promised Sammy I would see her. I will keep that promise. I can promise no more.'

That appeared to satisfy Mother. She turned to her eggs and began to beat them again, hard and fast, but already the bottom of the skillet had turned brown and hard.

'Go on, get back in there and eat your breakfast. You know I hates people in my kitchen. Go on now. Get.'

His food had cooled, but he ate, washing down the biscuits and gravy with two cups of coffee.

Once more outside, the wind struck him like a sharp knife, cutting through his coat and pants, bringing with it the smell of old snow from the high valleys and peaks where packs lay thirty and forty feet deep. However, the sun spent more and more time breaking through the clouds, warming the earth. Already placer miners had resumed their work in valleys and on hillsides, scratching the earth for the elusive yellow dust. Success lay just a few inches below the surface and all they had to do was dig. If they failed to unearth it right away, then dig a little deeper, until at last the future was theirs. Or so they believed.

Those men were already too late. To reach the dust of dreams, they would have to enter the bowels of the earth itself. That wealth lay in the hands of those who controlled the Bodie Mine or the smaller Molly B, entrepreneurs like Mr Lott, men capable of investing a great deal of hard cash for machinery and labor. The little man was squeezed out, although that realization remained elusive for many.

How could Josh oppose a man like that, a man he respected and a man whose daughter he courted? He would tell Rosa May that she must find someone else to champion her. Despite the protestations of Sammy Chung and Mother Mapes, Josh owed the girl nothing except a courteous denial.

He had seen this Rosa May many times around town. At least on three occasions he had met her coming out of Sammy Chung's house. He had to admit, her face haunted him, especially her smile, which was little more than a sweet upturning of her lips.

Josh cursed himself. What foolishness, thinking about a whore in that way. She once offered him a smile. So what? She was a whore who gave her smiles freely in order to bring a higher price for her body.

He wandered up Main Street toward the saloons, which, even at this early hour, kept their doors open for business. Behind those dens of iniquity, lay other, more degrading and cruel dens of iniquity, Virtue Lane. As Mother Mapes so accurately noted, he had never visited the place. In fact, he had never seen one of their shacks up close.

He turned down a worn path beside the Emporium that took him to the ramshackle huts where the whores serviced their customers. He was unsure of his motives, except he thought himself curious. He simply wanted to see the kind of environment in which Rosa May Whitefield worked.

What he saw appalled him. Mother Mapes was right about the cabins. They were nothing more than wood frame structures, many with gaping holes between planks. He passed one whose door had blown open. Light sliced through the warped wood, and the wind whistled through cracks like a beckoning ghost. A single bed lay pressed against the far wall, its uncovered mattress soiled and stained. The room smelled of whiskey and stale sex.

Disgusted, Josh hurried back to Main Street. He passed the front of the Emporium and crossed to the jail. He struck the door and heard boots scrape against the floor. Grey asked, 'Who is it?'

'Joshua Thorn,' he answered.

Grey lifted the bar and opened the door. 'This is going to cause you a hell of a lot of trouble.' He spoke softly and without rancor.

Josh walked past to the cells. Here, the early morning light was kept at bay by closed shutters across barred windows, a feeble attempt to keep out the cold. With each breath, a white cloud rolled out of his mouth. Chilled, he hugged his coat tighter. The cold penetrated more deeply here, penetrated right to the bone. The cold of the grave, he thought.

She sat on her cot, huddled within a couple of wool blankets. The swollen left eye and cheek were already turning brown. Her bottom lip was cut and swollen. When she looked up, her eyes appeared lifeless, dull. He had seen that look in others, all men in the same position as she, men who knew they were dead. To make it official, all they needed was for the traps to open, the bodies to drop, the necks to snap.

'Sammy Chung sent me,' Josh said.

She smiled, but the smile held no humor. 'It is a waste of your time. I told Sammy that. Please, Mr Thorn, go away before I ruin your life, too.'

'You look as if you got little sleep last night,' he said, and realized the absurdity of the comment.

'I fear I will never sleep again, except in death,' she said. 'I feel no remorse for what I did. My only regret is that I failed to kill Gunderson Lott, too.'

Leaning into the bars, Josh spoke in a low whisper. 'Don't say that. Don't ever say that again. If you do, you will be putting a noose around your neck for sure.'

'I am condemned, and nothing can change that,' she said.

He gripped the bars, trying to steady himself. He was allowing himself to be drawn into this mess, and his only chance was to back out now. To leave as she suggested, run out of the door and flee this stupid, destructive situation. Instead, he said, 'As long as we live, there is hope. We must cling to that.'

'Hope brought me to Virginia City, and it brought me to Bodie. It has been my constant companion, and yet I am here.' She allowed her eyes to examine the cell. 'This is as good as any place to end it. Better than any saloon I have worked. I have blankets to keep me warm. There are no men to paw me every second. I have a few days of peace before they hang me. So put your hope away, Mr Thorn, and let me be.'

She pulled the blankets more tightly around her as if to signal the conversation ended. Josh wanted to tell her how sorry he was, not just for her incarceration but for her life, miserable as it was, but he found no words of comfort. He tried to think of a Biblical passage to give her comfort, but even that failed him.

He walked away, but before he reached the door, her

voice, soft and sincere, floated from her cell. 'It was kind of you to come, Mr Thorn.'

Josh felt an immense wave of guilt as he stepped into the warmth of the outer office.

Grey stood by the front window, his thumbs curled into his belt. He watched Josh cross to the door, and as usual, he remained still and silent.

Outside, the wind struck Josh with its full force, but he thought it warmer than among the cells. Then with a sudden and overpowering rush, so strong it was like a physical blow, he felt the need of a drink. He headed across the street to the Emporium, and once inside, went to the bar where he ordered a whiskey. When he lifted the glass, he discovered his hand shaking. Some of the whiskey spilled over the lip, spotting the counter. He was shaken by her beauty as well as his desire to help.

'Thorn, you son-of-a-bitch!' The voice boomed from the door.

Deputy Lauter crossed the floor. He was two or three inches taller than Josh and outweighed him by at least forty pounds. As if to emphasize his size, Lauter swelled his chest with air. He stepped in close, his burly chest pressing against Josh.

'You went to see the whore! I saw you coming out of the jail. Goddamn you!'

On more than one occasion, Josh and Lauter butted heads. On his first day in Bodie, Josh stopped the deputy from beating a Chinaman, and Lauter had hated him ever since.

Josh stared at the mirror behind the bar, watching himself as if in a dream, unfamiliar and distancing.

'She killed Smith and nearly did the same to Gunderson. Gun's my friend. Now she must pay for it, and no lawyer with all his tricks is going to get her off.'

32

Looking at the image of the big man, Josh said, 'I am not representing her. I went there to tell her. Now leave me alone and let me have my drink.'

Lauter narrowed his eyes as he studied Josh's face. With a thick finger, he poked Josh on the shoulder.

'We will hang the little whore, and I am going to be there to make sure it happens. You hear me, Sky Pilot? Get in my way, and I will step on you like I would a cockroach.'

Left alone, Josh laid his empty glass on the bar and dropped a half-dime beside it. He needed no false courage to warp his judgment. He wanted to be as alert as possible when he faced Susan and the Lotts. The visit to the Emporium was only a momentary slip into past transgressions.

4

Even before Josh reached the front door, it opened, and Lott stepped out, his face red and splotchy with suppressed anger. Susan came to the door and stood behind her father. Josh paused at the foot of the stairs and looked up at the heavy-chested man.

'You went to see the little strumpet who ruined Gunderson,' Lott said.

Things were going to get very ugly if he failed to make his position clear. Yet some stubbornness held him back, an unwillingness to give in, to be bullied. The old man tried to intimidate Josh with a hard stare, the same he had tried the night before when he demanded Josh come to work for him.

'Why the hell did you do it, Josh?' In the midst of all his fury, the old man sounded wounded. 'If you insist on defending this whore, you are through in this town. I will see to it.' The old man lifted a fist. 'Get away from me and mine before I take a horse whip to you.'

Josh looked into the eyes of the old man and spoke softly although he felt himself on the edge, ready to lash out. 'I came here to explain, but I can see it is a useless gesture.'

Josh turned and descended the stairs. Behind him, Lott said, 'Damn you to hell, Joshua Thorn.'

Without looking back, Josh headed up Main Street. For almost a year he had courted Susan. During that time, he had eaten dinner with the Lotts every Wednesday and

Sunday. He attended church services with them, prayed with them. He worked with Mr Lott and the city council in planning activities like the spring cotillion and the July 4th parade. Twice he drafted city ordinances, the first in an effort to control saloon hours along lower Main Street, the second to keep the use of opium restricted to the Chinese population. By now Lott should have known Josh well enough to understand.

As he walked, men spoke greetings, but Josh, so lost in his own anger and frustration, failed to acknowledge them. Only when Reverend Warrington stepped out of the Pioneer Boot and Shoe and blocked his path did he stop.

'Joshua, my boy. So good to see you today.' Under one arm the pastor clutched a pair of freshly polished boots. He held out his other hand as a greeting.

Josh took the offered hand. 'Good day, Pastor.'

The pastor was very thin, his hand bony and hard.

'I attended to the Lotts this morning to offer my condolences and to pray with them.'

Reverend Warrington said a tsk-tsk-tsk and shook his head. As he did so, the wind fluttered his muttonchops.

'Terrible about poor Gunderson. Just terrible. I tell you, my boy, Bodie is a sea of sin. I hear the perpetrator is in jail. A woman of ill repute. But justice will be served. The good Lord will see to that.'

'I suppose,' Josh said, but his tone was non-committal and distant.

The pastor raised an inquisitive eyebrow. 'You do believe she deserves punishment. After all, a man died here. And what she did to Gunderson! Why, such action should appall every decent man and woman in Bodie.'

'Sounds like you advocate a little Old Testament vengeance, Pastor,' said Josh.

Reverend Warrington flashed an indulgent smile.

'Remember what Isaiah said: "Let the wicked forsake his way, and the unrighteous man his thoughts." Sound advice for us all, Joshua.'

A gust of cold wind sliced into his neck and face. Josh pulled his collar up around his ears.

'You know I saw the girl this morning.'

'The word is all over town. But, son, do you think it right to defend a person such as this?' He pursed his lips together as if he had a particularly bad taste in his mouth.

'What happened to Christian charity, Pastor? And innocent until proven guilty?'

'Oh, she is guilty, my boy. We have too many witnesses to doubt that. Any trial will be a formality at best.' He laid a hand on Josh's shoulder, a gesture obviously meant to impart a sense of cordiality and trust. Josh stiffened at the touch. The pastor saw this, but it failed to dissuade him. 'What is best here, I believe, is to get this business behind us and get on with our lives.'

'You think that best for the girl, too?' Josh shook off the pastor's hand. Up until this moment, he tolerated Reverend Warrington because the man preached the word of God, but his stiff-necked prudery had always irked Josh. The man had no sense of forgiveness or generosity for those who strayed. Now Josh discovered with a bitter finality, he despised the man. Through tight lips, he said, 'The road to salvation is a difficult one, Pastor. For all of us.'

He stepped around the pastor and continued up Main Street.

He had little idea where he was headed. He walked in a fog of anger, one so pervasive, so consuming that he recognized no one, saw nothing. Far down lower Main Street a shot rang out, and he acknowledged it as one might acknowledge the buzz of a fly, forgetting about it even before the echo died. All he could hear were the words of Lauter, Lott

36

and the pastor as they told him what to do. Somewhere behind those faces lurked the image of Susan.

Shocked, he discovered he stood before the jail. Without considering the consequences, he beat his fist against the door.

The door opened, and Lauter filled the narrow entrance.

'What the hell?' He glared at Josh with such hatred that a vein on his right temple rose to life and beat with a cadence all on its own. 'You have no business here, Sky Pilot.'

'I will see my client,' said Josh.

Lauter continued to block the doorway.

'Get out of my way, Lauter.'

Lauter twisted his lips into a snarl. 'Make me,' he said.

The big man wanted to fight. Josh stood rooted. If he must take a beating, he would do so, but he would be damned if he allowed Lauter to run him off. Once that happened, Lauter would forever have the upper hand, and Josh would be finished in Bodie.

'Let him in,' Grey said from inside.

His jaw was firmly set, Lauter glared over his shoulder at the marshal. 'Listen, you son-of-a-bitch, he ain't gettin' near that whore. He ain't using any of his lawyer tricks to get her off.'

A hand grabbed the back of Lauter's coat and pulled him away from the door. Lauter spun on the marshal, his shoulders hunched as if he were about to take a swing. Lauter froze. Grey had drawn one of his Colts and pressed the barrel against Lauter's belly. The weapon was cocked.

'I will allow no man to call me that.' Grey spoke very softly, but his voice held a cold rage.

A week before, Grey had killed a man. A drunk miner had cornered Mr Lott late one evening on Main Street as Lott strolled home from the Bodie Mine. The miner drew a pistol and even managed to fire a wild shot that nicked the hitching post near Lott. From thirty yards, Grey dropped the miner with one shot that pierced his heart and lungs. By the time Josh arrived on the scene, the man lay dead in the mud. The dark red that covered his chest merged with the black mud of the street.

Lauter understood the danger he faced, and he offered no resistance. With his free hand, Grey plucked the badge from Lauter's coat, leaving jagged and broken threads in its wake.

'Get out.' Grey forced the big man back through the door.

Lauter stood on the walk, his hands held before him. 'Come on, Grey. I lost my temper. I meant nothing by it.' His face and tone had lost all defiance. He appeared contrite and hurt, like a dog scolded by its master. Then, his snarl returned. He pointed a finger at Josh. 'That bastard—'

'Blame only yourself for what happened.' Grey motioned for Josh to enter. He kicked the door closed and dropped the bar into place, sealing the room. Angrily, he stuffed his revolver in its holster and turned on Josh. 'Does that satisfy you? Lauter no longer works for me.'

He stomped to his desk where he fell into a chair and stared at the wanted posters spread out on the desk. Josh was unsure whether Grey was angry with Lauter or with him. He knew better than to ask.

Rosa May still huddled on the bunk with the blankets drawn up around her neck, but she had opened the shutters wide enough to allow light to cut into the darkness. This time she appeared genuinely surprised to see him.

The cell was cold, but he unbuttoned his coat. The cool air refreshed him.

'Why have you come back?' she asked.

'Too many people ordered me to stay away.'

Her expression showed confusion, yet also a glimmer of

gratitude. Then, the spark died, and her eyes returned to the land of the dead. Rosa May Whitefield leaned back against the wall and pulled at the blanket in an effort to shrink beneath it.

'I deserve my fate, whatever it may be.' Then with a finality as heavy as lead, she said, 'I wanted to kill them all.'

'Why?' he asked. 'Help me to understand.'

'You know who I am, what I am. Even if I tell you, it will make no difference.'

'Give me a chance,' he said. 'I will not judge you.'

'Everybody judges everybody.'

Her tone remained soft, but the accusation stung him.

'I suspect the same people who passed judgment on you have since done so on me. Sammy Chung is my friend. Trust me when I say I have suffered grief over that. I have also suffered grief over my earlier visit to you.'

'We all have our crosses to bear,' she said.

'Tell me about your cross,' Josh said. 'The one you carry right now. I want to hear. I need to hear.' When she remained silent, her eyes fixed on the dark wall, he said, 'Miss Whitefield. Please.'

She lifted her eyes. 'You called me Miss Whitefield. Except for Sammy Chung, no man calls me that.'

'Do you object?' he asked.

'The last time a man called me Miss Whitefield, I was fourteen and attending Mrs Starkfield's School for Girls. I had just learned to waltz.' She smiled as she remembered that other life so far away in the vast fields of that dark republic. 'I was very graceful then.'

'You are still graceful,' Josh said.

Her face turned hard and stony. 'Sweet talk will get you nothing in here, mister.'

'It was only an observation. Nothing more.' Josh leaned forward against the bars. 'Just tell me what happened.'

In an unemotional tone, she told her story. As she spoke, he saw the events through her eyes, and in doing so, discovered heat rising along the back of his neck, a bad sign. Anger often led him into dangerous and unpredictable acts. He kept telling himself to listen to the facts, find his defense. When at last she finished, she closed her eyes as if trying to hide from the images that haunted her.

'Who will think it matters what they did to me?' she asked.

'It matters to me,' Josh said.

She shook her head. Black locks tumbled across her forehead. 'If you try to defend me, you will lose.'

'I will not burden you with false hopes,' he said. 'The odds are against us. Most in this town have already made up their minds.'

'I am guilty. I shot Gunderson. I killed that other man. So what if they forced themselves on me?'

His jaw tightened, and his cheeks burned. 'No woman deserves what they did to you.'

'Not even a whore, Mr Thorn?'

'No, ma'am.' He placed his elbows on the cross bars so that his whole body weight leaned toward her. 'I want you to tell me about yourself. Tell me everything.'

'How will that help?' she asked.

'I don't know that it will,' he said, 'but I need to hear. Perhaps there is something. . . .'

She was born in Bluffton, Ohio, in April of 1861, the same month Confederate General Beauregard opened fire on Fort Sumter. The war barely touched her family. Her father, a banker's son, paid $300 for a substitute and spent the next four years wasting his time teaching himself to paint. He was too lazy to learn his craft well. As a result, he found himself drawn to other pursuits, mostly women. Mrs Whitefield, a petite woman built much like Rosa May, discovered that heavy doses of brandy made her life bearable. As a result, Rosa May spent most of her youth in the care of nurses. When she was old enough, her parents shuffled her off to Mrs Stark's School for Girls in Cincinnati. She returned home only on Independence Day and Christmas.

The proprietress at the school taught Rosa May all the proper etiquette for dining and dancing and socializing in acceptable company. She taught her to sew and dress so that she would appear attractive and pleasing to men. She taught her to play the piano and to read poetry aloud.

In effect, she taught Rosa May and the other girls everything they would need to make a prosperous man happy and content. She failed to teach her young wards the cruelties that life could perpetate. Within the walls of the school they lived cloistered existences like young novices, but once free of those restraints, many of the girls learned other things.

In July of 1875 as she neared fifteen, she returned home for one of her few visits. She arrived on a Saturday evening, and already the celebration was in full swing. As the public coach passed the Stars and Stripes Inn, Rosa May pushed aside the curtain to witness a half-dozen men raising mugs in a toast. Up the street, patriots fired off shots at the last rays of day. Children ran along the walks, sparklers gripped in their little fists. The front of each store displayed Old Glory, either hanging above the doors or plastered to the windows.

Although she was tired and hot from the trip, she had trouble containing her excitement. She loved this day above all others because people celebrated it with such unbridled enthusiasm. All year long she lived in a staid and controlled environment, but this one day she saw people at their most uninhibited, and it gave her a sense of possibilities.

One of the black servants met her at the post office and drove her to her house. By the time she arrived, downstairs was filled with more than thirty of the best people in town

41

enjoying the free food and wine. A few relatives on her father's side were also in attendance, including Cousin Samuel, whom the family regarded as somewhat of a cad because of an incident with a certain young lady.

Her father, surrounded by a small crowd, nodded in her direction but otherwise ignored her. Her mother was absent, probably in her room imbibing brandy and awash in self-pity. Rosa May hurried off to her own room where she washed the dust from her hands and face and changed into a clean dress. Over the past year, most of her baby fat had disappeared. In its place was a trim waist and developing breasts. Before she left her room, she applied a touch of rouge to her lips and pinched her cheeks to give them color.

As she descended the stairs, a fan held delicately in her right hand and shading the lower part of her face, she could not help but notice the stares she elicited from the men. Even Cousin Samuel paused to watch her, his eyes alive with a rakish humor. For the first time in her life, she felt the power of being a woman, and the realization made her a bit lightheaded. By the time she reached the bottom of the stairs, the Grieg brothers, Bluffton's most eligible bachelors, were there to greet her.

'May I say how lovely you look this evening, Miss Whitefield,' said Lewis, the older by less than two minutes. Befitting his advanced age, he stood several inches taller than his brother. Other than the fact they were both red-heads, they shared few physical characteristics. Lewis certainly had the more impressive build, but Jared, the younger, possessed the better looks.

Hanging to the arm of each brother, Rosa May entered the library, her face aglow with the sudden attention thrust upon her. With a raised eyebrow, her father noted her changed appearance. Her mother, who had come down since her arrival, crossed the room and kissed her on the cheek. Rosa May smelled the brandy on her breath, but she smiled and said she was happy to be home. The three-piece band, two violins and a piano, struck up 'The Blue Danube', a waltz by Johann Strauss, who was beginning to find his mark in America.

Rosa May danced beautifully, just as Mrs Starkfield had instructed her, and she could tell from the way the men regarded her that they found her more than an acceptable companion. When Cousin Samuel finally captured her for a turn, he held her a little too close and a little too tight than decorum allowed. With his cheek near hers, he whispered, 'You have made many conquests tonight, my dear. Why, who would have thought it?'

The combination of the heat and the dancing and the wine gave her the impression that other dancers swirled in mist. Soon it seemed as if only she and Samuel remained on the floor, moving in such synchronization that they were one. Older than her by seven or eight years, he had for so long kept his distance, a relative who occasionally graced their house with social calls. He had had little time for a skinny girl who was all legs and whose head was full of dolls and silly romance.

Since the first time she discovered her interest in boys, she had fantasized about Cousin Samuel, who despite his reputation, cast a romantic glow over her girlish dreams. Now he held her in his strong arms, and when he looked into her eyes, she saw the desire that burned there.

Later, although she could not exactly remember when or how, they found themselves alone in the garden and seated on a stone bench. Samuel and she were kissing, and his hands roamed over her breasts. She knew she should tell him to stop, but she could barely breathe, and the effort to speak was entirely too great. In the midst of all her befuddlement, she agreed to an assignation the next day.

A week later, Samuel showed up in Cincinnati with a rented rig from the local livery. Just past midnight he carried her two bags down the back stairs of the school, threw them in the rear of the buggy. They drove away in the dark, her arms clasping his so tightly that he had to ask her to ease up.

'Where will we be married?' she asked.

'We need to get as far as way as possible before that old woman who runs the school has the law after us.'

They rode on in the dark night with only the sound of the hoofs of the matched pair striking the bare ground. She wanted to say so much, to tell Samuel of all the things she was feeling, but his stiffness was like a wall. Occasionally she glanced back to see if anyone followed, but the night was so black that, even if someone were there, she would never have seen him. When Samuel finally broke the silence, he said, 'I think our destination is west to Virginia City. I have heard money is to be made there, and all it takes is a man who can use his brains. We will be rich in no time.'

Of course, he never married her. When they crossed the state line, he said they had to keep moving because he was sure the law was right behind. Calling themselves Mr and Mrs Walton, they joined a wagon train in Omaha. The journey across the plains and desert was hard, but Samuel, who despised manual labor, managed to remain optimistic. He knew at the end of their journey lay the fortune he so richly deserved.

By the time they rolled into Virginia City, their funds were almost exhausted, and Rosa May was three months pregnant. Samuel soon discovered that making his fortune was not easy as he supposed. There were no nuggets lying around the street to be scooped up and converted to cash. The only jobs available were for those willing to go into the mines and hack at the hard ground with backbreaking intensity.

Social position in Virginia City was clearly defined. At the top of the hill resided the wealthy, those who owned and controlled the mines. Below them lived the managers and bureaucrats. On the next level lived the miners and workers. At the very bottom lived whores and gamblers and anyone else of low class. Here Samuel found a shack, so in need of repair that he had to nail up loose planks to keep the wind from plowing through gaping holes.

Rather than spoil his hands, Samuel turned to wagering at three-card Monte, fan-tan and poker. At first he won more than he lost. He was able to keep food in their bellies, but in the winter, his luck turned. Soon he began to operate on chits, and his ability to control his temper eroded as his confidence eroded.

Twice when she criticized his gambling, he beat her, the second time so badly she lost the baby and almost died. When she recovered, he mumbled an apology, yet she was certain he was glad there was to be no child.

Luck continued to elude him, and men about the city began to make threats. One night when the snow was deep and the wind sliced through the cabin like knives of ice, he told Rosa May that he had found her a job. The next evening she was to begin work at Madame Mustache's Emporium.

'You want me to wait tables?' she asked.

He looked away at the stove where a few coals still glowed through the grate. 'No money in that.'

She understood what he meant.

'I am a dead man, if you don't.'

She no longer loved him, not after what he had done to her and the baby. Maybe she even wished him dead. Yet, the next night, frightened and alone, she entered her new life.

Less than a month later, two miners caught Samuel dealing from the bottom of the deck and shot him dead. By then it was too late. Rosa May was trapped.

'I came to Bodie thinking things would be different. I was wrong. The only thing different is the winters are colder.'

'What about going home?' Josh asked. 'Did you ever consider that?'

'I have nothing to go back to. My father never cared what I did, and my mother has her bottle to keep her happy. I doubt they even remember me.'

She slumped back against the wall and turned her face toward the shadows. Josh feared she was about to cry, but she kept herself under control. For that, he admired her. Women who cried made him uncomfortable.

Still, he wanted to slip his arm around her shoulders, to comfort her, but the iron bars separated them, which was just as well. She would see it as an effort on his part to take advantage of her, and he was determined to keep their relationship strictly lawyer-client.

'It is the nature of my job to ask questions, Miss Whitefield. Sometimes I seem to ask stupid questions or questions that I have no right to ask. For that, I apologize, but they are necessary.' He had bothered her enough for one day, and he feared he had tired her. 'Is there anything I can get for you?'

'Could you bring me a book? It would help pass the time.'

'What would you like?'

'Jane Austen. I have not read her in years. *Sense and Sensibility* or *Emma*. I know I am asking a great deal—' She shrugged, and the look of resignation returned to her face. 'I doubt many in this town have ever read Jane Austen.'

'I will see what I can do,' Josh said, but he suspected that she was right. Bodie was not a place where Jane Austen would reside.

5

Josh pushed through the swinging doors of the Emporium and went to the bar and ordered a beer. Cain drew a pint and slid the mug along the counter. He continued to stare at Josh with dark, hollow eyes that lay so deeply within his skull they were mere slits that reflected no light. Josh tried to fathom what the man was thinking. Cain was an enigma. His expression revealed nothing.

Josh leaned forward, his elbows on the counter. As he had done earlier that morning, he studied himself in the mirror behind the bar. Dark stubble covered his cheeks and jaw, and the flesh under his eyes hung heavy and red. Even his neatly trimmed mustache appeared to droop.

A figure emerged from his left, his big bulk hunched like a bear ready to attack.

'You son-of-a-bitch, I told you—' Lauter grabbed Josh by the shoulder and spun him around.

Josh whipped the mug across Lauter's face. The heavy glass, full of beer, cracked into his cheek with a hollow thud so powerful that it snapped the big man's head to the right. Lauter staggered back, his legs beginning to buckle. Josh brought the mug straight down on the top of Lauter's head. The glass shattered. Lauter groaned and dropped to his knees. Blood flowed in a stream from under his hat.

47

His weight going forward, Josh threw a punch from the shoulder, his fist plowing into Lauter's nose and cheek with a solid impact that radiated all the way up his arm. Lauter toppled backward, his body twisting with the blow.

But Lauter was not out. He sat upright and wiped his face with his sleeve, smearing blood across his crushed lips and nose. 'Damn you—'

Josh waited until Lauter was almost on his feet before he struck again, a solid left to the nose. When Lauter raised his hands to protect his face, Josh plowed into his belly, three quick, solid blows. Josh heard the whoosh of air from Lauter and smelled his rancid breath. Lauter tried to grab Josh, his fingers scraping the hard wool coat.

Josh shot his knee into the big man's groin. Lauter grabbed his crotch, and his eyes rolled back in his head. He toppled to the floor. Dropping a knee into Lauter's chest, Josh drove a fist into his face and then another and another. Lauter was past protecting himself. The blows landed unimpeded, smashing into the cheekbones and nose and mouth with such ferocity that, with each blow, blood showered both participants and spotted the sawdust.

Behind Josh, someone shouted, 'You're gonna kill him!'

The words penetrated his burning rage. In the middle of a blow, his fist drawn back, Josh understood how far he had gone. Rubbing his raw knuckles, he searched the faces of those within the room, but the bearded miners and drifters stared back, stilled by the sudden explosion of violence.

Lauter's thick body jerked like a man with palsy. With each expulsion of breath, his lips blew bright blood.

Standing over the fallen man, Cain wiped his bony hands with a dishtowel.

'By God, you have ruined him.' His voice carried a tone of admiration.

For the first time since he entered the saloon, Josh felt

the heat. The air above the iron stove shimmered in undulating waves. Pools of sweat gathered under his arms, and his heart beat furiously.

A voice, silent but nevertheless powerful, told Josh that he should finish the job. Kill Lauter before Lauter had a chance to kill him. But the fight had drained Josh of his anger. He despised Lauter, but Josh was no cold-blooded killer. He stepped past the fallen man and walked out of the saloon into the mid-morning air.

A breeze had sprung up since he had entered the Emporium and carried a hint of spring warmth. Then, without warning, the wind turned mean, swirling cold into his damp shirt and reminding him that winter had yet to surrender. He buttoned his coat and hurried back to his office.

Even as he climbed the stairs and reached the landing, he wanted to return to the jail to see Rosa May Whitefield once more. She was a prostitute, a Jezebel who sold her body for money, and he believed he should feel some guilt, some remorse, for this attraction. Yet he could muster none. Even with her bruised and swollen face, she was lovely and desirable.

He opened the door and entered his office.

'Josh.' Susan threw herself against him with such force that it knocked him back a step. He barely had enough sense to kick the door shut so that no one outside would see them. She wrapped her arms around his neck and kissed him, her mouth open, her lips moist, her breath hot. Abruptly, she broke away and faced him. 'Why did you do it, Josh? Why did you go to see that woman? And after what she did?' Before he could answer, she said, 'And then you came to our house. I could have slapped your face.'

Josh leaned against the door. 'Sammy Chung asked me to see her.'

'You could have turned him down. You could have

refused to defend this woman.'

'That is exactly what I was about to tell your father this morning. I visited the girl as promised, but I told her that she would have to find someone else to defend her. If your father would have listened, I would have told him.'

Susan brightened, and her eyes filled with love and promise. 'We must go to Father right now. You must explain. If he knew this, why—'

'I will explain nothing to your father, not now. Anyway, it is too late.'

Her brow wrinkled in confusion. 'Too late?'

'I have agreed to defend her.'

'But that whore shot Gunderson and killed another man. Have you forgotten that?'

'Of course not, Susan. I know exactly what she did and why she did it.'

She lifted a hand to her throat as if she were about to suffer an attack of the vapors, one of her little tricks she employed when she was intent on getting her way. 'We can never be together if you do this.'

He knew she was right. It was the end of 'them,' if there was ever a 'them.' Yet, while Susan was quite desirable and a marriage with her would mean a secure future, he felt no qualms, no pangs of regret, no sense of loss. If anything, he experienced a sense of liberation.

Why? he asked himself.

But he knew the answer. The image of Rosa May Whitefield stood between them. He ached with pain when he thought of her.

He turned the knob of the door, opening it, and a blast of cold air burst into the room.

'You are a wonderful girl, Susan. You will be much better off without me.'

'You are throwing away everything we have. No man in his

right mind—'

'I'm not in my right mind. Leave it at that.'

Josh took her by the arm and guided her through the door. As she passed he smelled her perfumed soap, a faint hint of lilacs. In the past, he had lain in his bed smelling it as it clung to his hands and face where his flesh had touched hers. Those nights he fantasized having his way with her, consummating their relationship. Now that scent failed to arouse him. He wanted Susan gone so he could be alone with his thoughts.

'I will not have this, Joshua Thorn. I have given myself to you—' She stomped her foot '—heart and soul, and now you tell me that I would be better off without you. I will not accept that.' She ran down the stairs where at the bottom she looked up at him. 'We will talk later after you come to your senses.'

The street was alive with horses and wagons. An occasional gust of wind swirled loose shards of snow and ice in their wake. Men gripped their hats and pulled their coats tighter. Susan fled up the street toward her home, passing so close to Sammy Chung that their shoulders appeared to brush. Three steps behind Sammy walked Mai Lin, her beautiful dark eyes also locked on the wooden walk.

Josh watched as Sammy and his daughter climbed the stairs. They entered the office, and Josh closed the door, shutting the wind outside. However, the cold had penetrated every corner of the small room. When Sammy Chung spoke, white frost clouded his lips. 'I fear I have once again been the instrument of distress.'

Stepping to the small stove, Josh opened the grate and shoved in kindling and a couple of logs. The fire had died to a handful of live coals, but the wood was old and dry. Within a minute, the fire crackled and spit.

When he straightened, Josh clasped his hands behind him and stood before the window from where he could see the Lott house. Susan was already out of sight.

A part of him, a very small part, wanted to rush to the Lotts and ask forgiveness, to plead momentary insanity, but when he conjured up the face of Rosa May, even that small doubt vanished.

He turned to Sammy. 'I make my own decisions. I attach no blame to you.'

Sammy gave a tiny bow. 'What do you think of Miss Whitefield's chances?'

'I know what those men did to her. I believe that she was justified.' With bitterness Josh added, 'However, I fear a jury will find her guilty, and she will hang.'

It was the first time he said aloud what he understood from the very first, and the act of saying it made the situation far more real and far more desperate. Yes, she was doomed unless he could deliver a miracle. The Bible was full of miracles, but he had never personally seen one, and he had no idea how to conjure one up.

Sammy said, 'Perhaps God will provide a way.'

'Whose god? Yours or mine?' asked Josh.

Sammy smiled. 'Ah, my friend, what does it matter so long as He hears and answers?' He kept his hands folded in front of him. 'I heard of the incident between you and Deputy Lauter.'

Josh felt the heat rise along the back of his neck. 'Lauter pushed me too far.'

'I understand your rage, but you must cage your temper. It will do neither you nor Miss Whitefield any good if you find yourself in trouble as you did in Dallas.'

'You know about that?'

A slight nod was Sammy's answer. 'Your temper has cost you a great deal already. What you do now, you must do with a cool head. You must think clearly and dispassionately.'

'I do not think I can save her,' Josh said.

'You must have more faith, my friend,' said Sammy.

'Faith in God?' asked Josh.

'Faith in yourself, my friend.'

Up to this point, Mai Lin stood off in a corner and remained silent, but she raised her eyes and said, 'Miss Whitefield care for Mai Lin when I cannot care for myself.'

He saw his own desperation mirrored in the eyes of the girl. 'I will do all I can,' he said.

In bed that night, he slept badly. When he did drift off, Rosa May haunted his dreams. A few minutes before four in the morning, he climbed out of bed and lit the lamp. Seeking comfort and guidance, he sat at his desk and opened his Bible to Psalms. While the words often provided solace, this morning they provided none. After fifteen minutes, he slammed the book shut. Sitting by the window, a blanket thrown across his shoulders, he watched as the dark sky turned pink.

Because of Gunderson's wounds, Judge Melrose postponed the trial until he was well enough to testify. In the meantime, Josh went to see Rosa May every day. As he suspected, he could uncover no copy of a Jane Austen novel, but on a back shelf of Dressler's General Store, he found a copy of *Uncle Tom's Cabin*. Passing it through the iron bars, he said, 'Sorry, but it is the best I could do.'

She opened the book to the title page and ran her fingers over the print as if she could feel the letters. She took a deep breath and settled back in the bunk.

'Thank you. You are very kind.'

Two days later, she had finished the book. By then, Josh had uncovered a complete edition of Shakespeare's plays, and this, too, he brought to her. She held the massive volume in both hands as if weighing it.

'No doubt you are familiar with the Bard,' Josh said.

'Yes. *The Tempest.*' She hugged the book and rocked back and forth. '*Taming of The Shrew. A Midsummer Night's Dream.*' Tears rolled down her cheeks, spotting the front of her plain, cotton dress.

She opened the book and began to read. Her bed lay diagonally to the bars, and he could see she chose Act V of *Romeo and Juliet.* Within moments she was blinded by her tears.

Feeling that this was a private moment, too private for his presence, he moved to leave.

Looking up, she said, 'Life is not always fair, is it, Mr Thorn?'

'Sometimes we can force our own brand of fairness on the world.'

'And is that what you intend to do?' she asked.

'To the best of my ability.'

'Then I wish us both luck, Mr Thorn, for surely we need it.'

'Yes, ma'am, we surely do.'

PART II

TO THE WESTERN MOUNTAINS

'From our own White Mountains, we can look across the valley to the green mountains capped by snow-covered peaks, those mountains we call the Sierra Nevada. Beautiful they may be, calling to us as the Sirens called to Odysseus, but let the unwary traveler be warned. Death lurks in those forested peaks and lush meadows, Nature's graveyard.'

—quoted in *The Weekly Bodie Standard*,
May 5, 1880

6

Carrying the canvas bag in his left hand and the Winchester over his right shoulder, Virgil Perry hurried down the gangplank, anxious to reach firm land. Forty-three days before, he boarded a ship in Galveston, and except for the week he and another dozen passengers spent crossing the insect-ridden Isthmus of Panama to connect with another ship, he had not touched land. With his feet safely upon the stationary dock, he found himself breathing more easily. He made a resolve then and there. He was through with the sea. For almost the entire voyage he had suffered a stomach sickness that kept him from keeping down food.

Reaching the end of the dock, Virgil easily picked out the man among the stevedores, merchant sailors and businessmen. Off to one side, he leaned against a dock post, his thumbs hooked over his gun belt. He stood well under five and a half feet, which made the pistol appear too large for him. Even when he stood upright, he appeared no more than a mouse of a man.

'I'm Bib Harkness,' the man said. 'I suppose you got a trunk or two that needs care.'

Virgil hefted the canvas bag. 'All I carry is here. We can be on our way.'

Harkness led the way through the Embarcadero.

'We leave first thing tomorrow morning,' he said.

'I prefer to leave immediately.'

'Tomorrow's the best I can do. As instructed, I purchased our gear, and it awaits us in Sacramento. However, the next train doesn't leave until nine tomorrow morning.'

Virgil grunted his displeasure. 'That will have to do, I suppose.'

They came to a street that followed the waterfront to a cluster of buildings a quarter of a mile away.

'We have rooms there.' Harkness nodded toward a two-storied building that sported an ornate false front full of golden curlicues surrounding the face of a woman. 'The Bella Donna. Best accommodations on the Barbary Coast. A sportin' man's paradise.'

'I am not a sportin' man,' Virgil said. He had hoped to be on their way, but instead he faced a night with revelers and mountebanks, a situation designed to put him in a foul temper.

'We will be on the road many days,' Harkness said. 'Tonight I aim to partake of my share of pleasures. It is a long and arduous road to Bodie. Once we leave Sacramento, we will be under the celibacy of the saddle.'

Virgil saw the futility of pursuing such a conversation. 'I was given to understand that you are a *pistolero* of some accomplishment and that you know this country.'

'That is true on both counts,' Harkness said.

'And Joshua Thorn.'

'I discovered his whereabouts last September, just before the snows came to the mountains. He has established a law office in Bodie.'

'Is he still there?' asked Virgil.

'Once the snows arrive, few people enter or leave the town. He was there when I left, and I barely beat the snow. We had a devil of a winter, and most of the passes are still closed. Likely he remains there.'

Virgil understood few things in this world held a guarantee, but this was more than satisfactory news. Thorn had fled Dallas over three years before, knowing that if he stayed, a dozen men would gun him down. Virgil soon learned Thorn boarded a wagon train in Santa Fe headed for California. He heard no more of Thorn until October of the previous year when he received a letter from Bib Harkness, who claimed he discovered Joshua Thorn resided in Bodie. The possibility existed, of course, that Harkness invented the story to cash in on the reward. Two others had tried it, but the only rewards they collected were unmarked graves. In this case, Harkness understood he was to be paid only when Thorn was dead.

As if he divined Virgil's thoughts, Harkness said, 'Ask anyone that knows me. They'll tell you that when Bib Harkness contracts for a job, he stays with it to the end. I have put up good money for our supplies, and I will consider that as my investment until the job is finished. You pay me then, expenses and all.'

Virgil shifted the weight of the rifle that burrowed into his shoulder. 'How long to Bodie?'

'We will reach Sacramento tomorrow night.'

'And after Sacramento?'

'Hard ridin' for a week, maybe more. Depends on the conditions of the trails. A long time for an anxious man.'

'I have waited three years,' said Virgil. 'I can shoulder another week or two.'

'And what makes this Joshua Thorn so important to you?'

Virgil remained silent, as they continued on the straight line toward the Bella Donna. He had little inclination to relate his history to this wisp of a man.

Harkness said, 'If I'm going to help kill a man, I deserve to know the reason.'

The point had merit, and Virgil said, 'Thorn killed my brother.'

Harkness remained quiet the rest of the way to the hotel. They passed many people on the street, sailors, gamblers, thugs, whores, but Virgil was too caught up in the memories of the past to give them more than a cursory glance. The only person he could see was Ike, dead these three years, his smiling face and lean, muscular body only an illusion.

Ike had arrived late in the life of Mother and Father, long past the time considered normal for couples their age. They believed that Virgil, already fifteen, was to be the last of their children, and their surprise was all the greater when they discovered Mother was carrying a child.

When Ike was born, he became their favorite, and like most couples who have a child late in life, they spoiled him badly. After all, the family had money. Father made a fortune hauling freight on the Trinity River. When they passed on, Mother five years after Ike arrived, Father nine months later, the task of raising the young boy fell to Virgil. Since women offered Virgil little temptation, he understood Ike was the closest he would ever come to having a son.

Often Virgil had warned Ike that pursuit of pleasure held dangers far beyond an occasional headache from too much liquor. Such actions, Virgil assured the kid, would eventually lead to trouble that family money might not solve. Ike only laughed and kept on doing as he always had.

Then came the woman, Beatrice Hale. Virgil would forever remember her name as well as Thorn's. Thorn and the woman were betrothed. But one afternoon on the streets of Dallas, Ike saw her and wanted her. He was a handsome devil. Ladies young and old said so. The fact that Miss Hale was engaged was of no consequence. If Ike had kept his mouth shut, had not felt the need to brag in the bars and saloons, then only he and the girl would have known. Once the story reached the girl, she realized she had comprised herself beyond all redemption.

In some ways, Virgil blamed himself. Perhaps had he tried to buy off Thorn, they might have avoided what followed. That was before they found the note that explained in great detail the reasons the girl had taken her life. She colored her reasons, making it sound as if Ike forced her. Maybe Ike had used a little extra persuasion, but forcing her ... That was an out and out lie. Women were all too willing to compromise themselves with Ike. The girl had tried to make herself appear more a victim than a willing participant. In that, she succeeded. Once the girl's family handed the note over to Thorn, he came looking for Ike.

The four witnesses agreed that Ike drew first and fired a wild shot that shattered the window of Peterson's Hardware. Slower on the draw, Thorn placed a well-aimed shot into Ike's breast and punctured the strong, young heart. Thorn calmly walked away and disappeared. The dozen men hired by Virgil to bring Thorn back, dead or alive, found only a trail that went cold in Santa Fe.

Now at last he felt close to the end. When this was over and Thorn lay dead, Virgil could again sleep through the night without seeing Ike lying in the street, his face covered with dirt so dark he took on the appearance of a minstrel show performer. No man deserved to look so comical in death, and Virgil hated Thorn for that indignity as much as killing Ike.

The mood of Bib Harkness had worsened each day since they had departed Sacramento seven days before. Virgil had put him in charge of the pack mule, and the stubborn animal constantly pulled against Harkness.

On this day, they traveled through a level valley. On their right rose the rugged Sierra Nevada where deep snows covered the high peaks and filled the passes. When the clouds came in from the coast, they deposited the bulk of their load on the Sierras, heavy with forests and lakes. By the time the clouds crossed the valley and met the White Mountains, they had little moisture left. As a result, these mountains were smoother and more rounded. Groves of trees were sparse and thin.

The valley in which they rode was lushly green. At noon they dismounted a few paces upstream from their horses. They knelt and cupped water in their hands and drank. For ten minutes they chewed beef jerky and worked the kinks out of their stiff bodies.

His hunger satisfied, Virgil grabbed a handful of grass, separating a clump with surprising ease. He rolled the grass and earth between his fingers as he surveyed the valley.

'Good cattle country,' he said.

They mounted their horses. With his spurs, Harkness gouged his mount and jerked on the line leading the pack mule. The animals leapt into the stream and crossed to the other side. Virgil followed.

'How far to Bridgeport, Mr Harkness?'

'We'll make it before sundown.' In a sour tone, Harkness added, 'This may look like good cattle country, but when winter comes, life is hard. People who live here do so because they are after gold or silver.'

'Is that why you came here?' asked Virgil. 'Frankly, I do not see you as a miner.'

'Some men find gold and silver in the ground. I find gold and silver in other men's pockets.' He patted his vest where a deck of cards outlined itself against the cloth.

'A chancy existence. Luck can turn against you,' Virgil said.

'Luck has little to do with the way I play cards,' Harkness said. 'And there is always work for a pistolero of my reputation.' Harkness shifted himself in the saddle to glare at Virgil. 'And you, sir, what are you?'

'Do not mistake me, Mr Harkness. I may wear fine clothes and appear a man of money, but I drove cattle herds to Sedalia in '68 and '69 and later to Abilene. I am trail hardened.'

'Ever use the .44 on your hip on anything larger than gophers and prairie dogs?'

'You ask a very personal question, Mr Harkness.'

Harkness spit, and a white stream flew into the tall grass. 'I ain't a prying man by nature, but tomorrow we'll be in Bodie. If we come across Thorn, there will be shooting. I must have confidence that the man covering my back has the wherewithal to pull down on a man.'

Virgil considered his answer before he nodded, the brim of his sombrero bobbing. 'I don't like to talk about such things. No reasonable man does. But you make a valid point. Let me put it this way. I never pushed a fight, but I never backed away from one either.'

'You're pushing this fight.'

The muscles in his neck and jaw tightened. 'Joshua Thorn laid my brother in his grave, and Ike barely twenty.'

Harkness shifted his weight so that he once again faced the trail ahead.

They entered Bridgeport with the sun beginning to drop behind the Sierras, giant shadows spreading across the valley floor. The town was composed of one wheel-rutted street with five buildings.

As they drew up before the Bridgeport Livery and Feed, Virgil said, 'There is another hour of daylight.'

Harkness dismounted and began to loosen the cinch of his saddle. 'We have a six or seven hour ride up the mountains to Bodie. I don't aim to spend the night on the trail if it ain't necessary. We best get a good night's sleep and allow the horses to rest.'

They ran their horses and the pack mule into the open corral and closed the gate. An old man showing a toothless grin took a silver dollar and shuffled off to rub down their mounts and provide feed. Virgil and Harkness crossed the muddy street to the Bridgeport Emporium and Saloon where a lower floor sported a bar and an upper floor housed rooms. While Virgil rented the last vacant room from the barkeep, Harkness cast his eye over a table at the back where four men bent over cards.

Virgil and Harkness climbed the dark stairs, and once in their room, dropped their saddle-bags beside the bed.

'Think I'll see about that game downstairs,' said Harkness.

'As you said, we have a long day ahead of us tomorrow,' Virgil said. 'I need your head clear.'

'I'm playing cards, not getting drunk,' said Harkness.

Virgil had never learned to appreciate cards. However, he was hungry, and tired of trail jerky and beans. He followed Harkness downstairs where he ordered a beer and ate pickled eggs from the tray at the end of the bar. His hunger abated, he ordered another beer and found an empty table against the wall from where he could view the card game.

Harkness had a small stack of silver dollars with a couple of gold coins thrown in. As he played, Harkness held the cards with a loose familiarity. His opponents were men whose faces were burnt dark by the sun, prospectors and miners who had spent too many years in the harsh Sierras and White Mountains. Their hands were big and rough, and they held the cards close to their chests and stared at them with a single-mindedness that made their faces easy to read. After half a dozen hands, Harkness found his pile of coins almost doubled.

Half past nine, one of the miners dropped out, leaving an

empty spot, and a young man slid into the vacated seat. Since entering the saloon twenty minutes before, he stood by the bar sipping his beer and watching the players. Now his turn had come. He was not a miner. He was clean-shaven except for a well-trimmed mustache, and wore a clean shirt and vest. His work pants and boots were those of a cowboy. Although he wore a pistol, an ancient Smith and Wesson .44, it rested too high on his hip, and a hammer guard held the pistol in place.

Smiling broadly, the young man slammed down a handful of silver. 'Deal me in, mister.'

Bib Harkness cast an irritated glance at the newcomer. The young man smiled and continued to smile with each hand. The smile itself was both distracting and disarming.

For the next hour, the majority of the pots were won by either Harkness or the kid. The two remaining miners soon lost their money and slunk off to the bar where they ordered beers. With only the young man and Harkness left, the kid began to scoop up his winnings.

'Enjoyed the game, mister,' he said.

A dark humor had settled over Harkness, the same dark humor that had been growing since they left Sacramento.

'You are an irritating piss ant.' Standing, Harkness flicked his coat so that the cloth rode away from his pistol, cloistered in a Mexican loop holster, one designed for the fast draw.

The bar turned still and silent as the kid stuffed money in his pants. His smile had grown tight and forced. 'Mister, I just came in for a friendly game. I want no trouble.'

He turned and headed for the door. Harkness was around the table and after him. 'Do not walk away from me.'

His smile wiped away, the kid faced Harkness. He tried to stand brave, puffing up his chest and narrowing his eyes. It was a pathetic bluff on the kid's part. Harkness ran a jaundiced eye up and down the slim figure.

'I ought to take away that .44 and spank you with it.'

The kid stood rigidly in place. 'You have no right to talk to me like that. I did nothing to you.'

The boy slid his hand toward the pistol, and Virgil thought that he was about to pull down on Harkness.

'Go ahead. I'm agreeable.' Harkness kept his voice soft and modulated.

The kid looked over to Virgil and then to the men at the bar.

'Mama and Papa ain't here to pull your chestnuts out of the fire, kid.' Harkness pointed to the door. 'Just git out of here while you can. And next time, keep out of men's games.'

The kid thought about it for only a moment before he spun away and pushed his way through the swinging doors.

Later in their room, Virgil said, 'You humiliated the boy.'

Harkness removed his boots, dropping them on the floor. He lay back, his arms under his head. 'The kid should have stayed out. It was my game. Not his.'

The next morning, they rose with first light, gathered their belongings and went downstairs where they finished the last of the pickled eggs. As they exited the saloon, they found the sun coloring the peaks of the western mountains, although the valley still lay in shadow.

Across the way, the kid sat with his back against the corral fence. When he saw them, he climbed to his feet. His eyes were red, and his clothes crumpled. He stepped forward, planting each foot carefully to keep from slipping in the muddy street. Ten feet away, the boy stopped and focused his attention on Harkness.

Harkness dropped his saddle-bags. His right hand brushed the butt of his .44. Sensing the danger, Virgil moved down the walk until he was almost at the edge of the building.

If shooting started, he wanted to avoid a stray bullet.

'You shamed me, mister,' the kid said.

Two wagons headed east drew rein twenty yards from the men, and the drivers sat watching. Across the street, the blacksmith ceased hammering and looked up. The old man who saw to the corral came and stood by the barn door.

'You owe me an apology,' said the boy.

The muscles of Harkness' jaw turned hard, and he stepped to the very edge of the boardwalk.

Virgil wished an end to this confrontation. He and Harkness had a far more important meeting in Bodie.

'Is an apology worth a killing?' Virgil asked the kid.

The kid glanced at Virgil, confusion evident in his eyes, but pride had driven him to this spot, and pride kept him planted in the middle of the street.

Harkness said, 'You lack the courage of a man. Otherwise, you'd stop whining and reach for your hog leg. Or is that just for show?'

The boy fumbled for his pistol. In one fluid movement, Harkness drew his .44, cocked it, and fired, the explosion rocking the porch under Virgil. The bullet thudded into the boy's belly. He gasped, frozen by pain and shock. Harkness fired again, so quickly the echo of the first shot still rang loud and clear. The second bullet struck the boy in the upper chest. Despite his wounds, the kid refused to surrender. Staggering to stay upright, he threw up his weapon. Two shots rang out. The boy's wild shot whined across the rooftops, and he tumbled forward into the muddy street. His body twitched once, twice, and he lay still.

The old man from the livery ventured into the middle of the street and kneeled beside the kid.

'He's still breathing,' said the old man.

Slowly, Harkness removed the spent cartridges and replaced them with fresh ones. With the pistol, he pointed to a bloody hole where with every breath, blood rushed out.

'My last shot got him through the lungs. That's why the blood is so dark.' He holstered his pistol. 'He ain't realized it yet, but he is dead.'

As if that were the signal, the boy sighed, and his muscles relaxed. His eyes remained open, but the light had gone.

The old man looked up at Harkness. 'Did you know him?'

'Played cards with him last night. Who was he?'

The old man shrugged. 'Been around town for a couple of days. That's all I know.'

'He has money he won last night,' said Harkness. 'Enough for burial. You take care of things, and you'll make a tidy profit, old timer.'

'I have done it before,' the old man said. 'Although it is not to my liking.'

When they had ridden a mile beyond town, Virgil said, 'The young man managed to get off a shot.'

Harkness spit. 'A wild shot.'

'A shot nevertheless,' said Virgil.

'An aberration. Nothing more.'

'In other words, you underestimated him. When we get to Bodie, do not make the same mistake with Thorn.'

Harkness laughed and shook his head. He was in a much better mood.

7

The day the trial began, Judge Melrose marched into Josh's office, swept his hat from his head and seated himself. He ran a knuckle across his white, flowing mustache, the right side first followed by the left

'Well, my boy, I must say that I am a bit disappointed. I hoped by now you would have made the proper moves to extricate yourself from this case. Have the girl admit her guilt and let us move on.'

Josh remained seated. 'As I see it, the fact that she shot the men is not the point.'

'Ah yes, motive. Was she justified in what she did?' The judge nodded. 'I am afraid the answer will bear little relationship to the outcome. People see only a woman of ill repute who has killed one man and tried to kill another, and that one, the son of our leading citizen. I am afraid you have hitched yourself to a dead horse, my boy. And I had such high hopes for you, Joshua.'

'Who else would defend her, Judge?' Josh tilted his chair back and his eyes drifted out of the window where a slow drizzle had moved in from the west. On the bluff, the Bodie Mine lay outlined in the mist. 'When I came here, you asked me to stay and represent the Chinese because they had no voice in the court. The Chinese are not the only ones without a voice.'

The judge leaned forward, planting one hand on Josh's desk. 'Your cause is hopeless. She will be found guilty, whether you defend her or not. You may still salvage your position here. I do believe the Lotts would welcome you back, if you gave them the chance.'

'I respect your advice, Judge. but we have reached a point where I must follow my conscience.'

The judge stood to go, but he paused at the door. 'This Rosa May has known many men. She is not worth the sacrifice, my boy.'

With that he was out of the door.

The trial was to begin at ten that morning. By 9.30, men filled every seat in the saloon and stood shoulder to shoulder along the walls. Among them sat eight or nine women, all whores. In the eyes of each, Josh saw the hint of fear. Each must have had a sense that in some small way she might be the one here on trial, if not for the crime of which Rosa May was accused, then another that could get her banished from town or worse.

During the past year, three whores were tried and found guilty of crimes, two for pinching pokes and another for attempting to kill a saloon owner who demanded a larger cut of her purse. Each was banished with a horse, the clothes on her back and enough food for five days. Once a whore was banished, she was finished. No other mining town or camp within a hundred miles would allow her to practice her profession within its borders. Often such a punishment was a death sentence, especially if enacted during the harsh winter months.

Josh caught sight of Lauter, his bruised face partially hidden behind a large, floppy hat. His small, pig-like eyes glared at Josh. By now everyone in town had heard of the beating Josh administered the man, and Lauter's reputation as a tough man had suffered. Men no longer feared him as they once had. If a man the size of Josh could do it, then anybody could.

In the front row sat Mr Lott and Gunderson. Mr Lott puffed on a cigar wedged between his teeth, and a cloud of smoke hung around his head, obscuring his features. Gunderson kept touching the heavy bandage that covered the left side of his face. His left shoulder was heavily taped, and his left arm rested in a sling.

Josh allowed his eyes to roam over the rest of the saloon. Sammy Chung, his arms folded inside his robe, stood near the rear door. Sing Tong, his right-hand man and body-guard, stood beside him. They were almost hidden by the crowd. Even the mere sight of Sammy raised Josh's spirits.

The old clock above the bar struck ten. The doors opened and Rosa May entered, escorted by Marshal Grey and Judge Melrose. They led her to the table. Josh rose and pulled out the chair next to him. Rosa May flashed a wan smile, but her eyes were heavy from lack of sleep. She wore a cotton dress buttoned to her neck. She wore no rouge to color her cheeks or lips. In this way, she was more strikingly beautiful than the first time he had seen her. Only the month-old remnant of the bruise on her cheek marred that beauty.

She folded her hands and kept her eyes toward the front. Lauter pushed his way through the crowd until he stood directly behind her, his voice raised so the whole room could hear.

'We got a plot all picked out for you, and I'll be the one shoveling dirt in your face.'

The cemetery on the outskirts of town was for decent residents only. The undesirables – whores, gamblers, drifters – were buried in a gulch a hundred yards beyond. The graves there were unmarked, and when the spring thaws came, especially in those years when the snow was high, the run off might rush right through the gulch and dig up the dead, spreading bones down the mountain and into the long valley between the White Mountains and the Sierras.

Lauter grabbed the girl roughly by the shoulder.

Angrily, Josh kicked his chair back and stood to face Lauter. Marshal Grey stepped between the two men. He spoke in a cold, measured voice. 'You give me one bit of trouble, Lauter, and I will finish the job Thorn started.'

Lauter swallowed, his thick Adam's apple bobbing. He faded back into the crowd.

The room had turned silent, and Josh, his face still heated, sat down. He laid a hand on Rosa May's and discovered her flesh cool to the touch.

Judge Melrose seated himself at the table on the raised platform. Removing the gavel from his coat pocket, he pounded the table once. The effect drew everyone's eyes to him. With the back of his hand, he stroked each side of his mustache. In his deep, booming voice he said, 'Mr Thorn, shall it be a jury trial? Or will you leave the decision to me?'

'A jury trial, Your Honor,' Josh said.

Judge Melrose nodded as if it were the correct decision. Legally Rosa May stood on weak ground. She had killed Smith and wounded Gunderson and Ash. The only course of action was to justify the shooting. If it came down to a matter of law, the judge would rule against her. In a jury trial Josh had to convince only one member of extenuating circumstances. A hung jury was as good as an acquittal because the judge had never once impaneled another jury after the first failed to reach a decision.

With his gavel, the judge pointed to the marshal. 'Gather names and draw from the hat to select the jury.' He turned his attention to Lott and his son. 'You gentlemen will, of course, excuse yourselves.' Raising his gavel higher, the judge pointed to the back of the room where Lauter had taken himself. 'And you, Mr Lauter, will not put your name in the hat. Is that understood?'

The judge struck the table once, very hard. 'I intend this trial to be conducted in an orderly fashion. Any outburst whatsoever, I will deal with in the harshest manner possible. Now I want all the smokes extinguished and the drinks put away. The bar is closed until these proceedings are concluded.'

Mr Lott removed the cigar from his mouth and looked at it with a tinge of regret before dropping it on the floor and grinding it under his heel. Others extinguished their cigars or pipes. When the barkeep opened a rear door, smoke swirled outside with the rain and mist. Other men downed the last of their drinks, and glasses clinked as waiters ran to collect them.

All this time, Marshal Grey scribbled names on slips of paper, folded them, and dropped each in his hat. He had collected more than thirty names. He shook his hat, dipped his hand into it and pulled out a slip.

'Shifty O'Connell.'

'Shifty' was a moniker, and Josh doubted that anyone in town knew the man's actual name, including Shifty himself. Many men in mining camps were known only by the monikers. O'Connell was called 'Shifty' not because people believed him dishonest or crooked but rather because of his eyes. Having spent too many years prospecting Death Valley, he had developed a permanent squint.

Bent with rheumatism, Shifty shuffled forward. Several years before he had given up prospecting, telling people he was too old for such work and had taken a job in the Bodie Mine as an assayer's assistant. As he passed Mr Lott, he cast a woeful glance in the direction of his employer as if to say he lacked any choice in this matter.

Marshal Grey drew eleven more names, and each man came forward to take a seat in the jury box. With the jury completed, Judge Melrose cast a stern eye on Josh. 'I assume you have no objection to any of these men, Counselor.'

Josh counted each and every one; like Shifty, they were either a miner or a merchant who owed allegiance to the mines. Still, Josh doubted that any other group would be more impartial than this one.

Josh rose to his feet. 'They are all honest men, Your Honor. I have no objections.'

'Quite right.' The judge nodded, and locks of his white hair tumbled across his forehead. He brushed them back. 'I think we can get on with the case, gentlemen. The charge, of course, is murder. Marshal Grey, you may begin.'

The marshal, who doubled as prosecutor, stood, his thumbs hooked into his gun belt.

'Yes sir, but I would like to suggest—'

'Your suggestion that the town hire a permanent prosecutor is once again noted.' With a wave of the gavel, he dismissed the objections. 'Present your case, Marshal.'

With a grunt of acceptance, Grey said, 'Gunderson Lott, come up here and take the stand.'

Gunderson stood close to six feet in height, and he was a healthy physical specimen, yet when he rose, his father held his arm and helped him to his feet. Gunderson shuffled to the stand, much in the same way Shifty O'Connell had done. Josh wondered how much was real and how much was show.

Once the judge administered the oath, Marshal Grey said, 'Now Gunderson, tell us what happened on the night of April 6th of this year.'

Gunderson fingered the bandage that covered the left side of his face, and his eyes darted to Rosa May. 'That whore put shot in my face and shoulder. Quarter an inch to the right and it would have taken my eye. Might have killed me.'

He tapped the heavy bandage. 'And this shoulder will never be right again.' As an afterthought, he said, 'She killed Smith. He was standing right next to me. He caught a full load in the chest. Tore the heart right out of his chest.'

'Were you threatening her in some way? With a gun or knife maybe?'

'No, sir. Not a one of us had our guns out. She came in blasting away.' He tapped his bandaged shoulder again. 'Meant to kill me. Meant to kill us all.'

'I object, Your Honor,' said Josh. 'The witness has no way of knowing what my client meant to do.'

Judge Melrose nodded his assent. 'Quite right. Please keep your remarks to facts, Mr Lott. Do not speculate on what other people might be thinking.'

Shifting his weight, Gunderson glanced sourly at the judge. 'She meant to kill me. That ain't speculation.'

'Where did she get this weapon, this shotgun?' asked Grey.

'Cain kept it behind the bar. It was a sawed-off double barrel Winchester.' The muscles in his face turned rigid. 'The whore had worked there for over a year. She knew its purpose.'

'Objection.' Josh jumped to his feet. 'Mr Lott has no knowledge that my client knew the purpose of this weapon.'

Before the judge could rule on the objection, Gunderson slammed his one good hand against the arm of the chair. 'She knew, goddamn it. Cain made sure everyone knew.'

'How can you be sure?' asked Grey.

Gunderson refocused his attention on the marshal. 'It was his way to discourage trouble in his place. Hell, I seen Cain use it once on a drifter causing trouble.'

'Will you rule on my objection, Your Honor?' Josh wanted to cut off this line of questioning.

The judge ran the back of his hand across his flowing

mustache. 'I think these questions are headed in the right direction. Now sit down, Mr Thorn. If I think Gunderson or the marshal strays from the point, I will set them straight.'

The marshal pushed his coat back and hooked his thumbs in his gun belt. 'You said you personally saw Mr Cain use the scattergun?'

'He didn't actually use it. He didn't have to. When Cain stuck the scattergun in the drifter's belly, that poor bastard wet his pants.' Gunderson laughed as he recalled the incident. 'If Cain had pulled the trigger, he would have cut that drifter in half. No man in his right mind would face a scattergun at close quarters.'

'And why do you think Rosa May Whitefield turned this scattergun on you and the others?' Grey asked.

'She had no reason. None. We were finished playing cards and about to head out of there. She's crazy if you ask me.'

Even before Josh had a chance to object, Judge Melrose slapped the table with the gavel. 'No more of that kind of talk.' To the jury he said, 'You men pay no attention. Gunderson Lott has no expertise to make such a judgment. You got any other questions, Marshal?'

'None that I can think of, Your Honor.'

When Josh stood, Gunderson leaned back in his chair, an arrogant smirk twisting his lips. Josh strolled to the front of the room, placing himself directly to the young man's right. Josh flashed a friendly smile.

'How do you feel today, Gunderson?'

'I'm all busted up. How do you think I feel?'

'Are you in much pain?'

Gunderson's brow came together in a question. 'Some. It grows worse at night.'

Josh nodded as if he understood. 'I suppose this has been a terrible ordeal.'

'My shoulder is busted, not to mention my—' He touched the bandage on his face.

'And you are angry about it. Real angry.'

'Damn right.'

'And you must hate my client for what she did to you. Hate her about as much as a man can hate anybody.'

Gunderson stared at Rosa May with eyes that answered the question. A vein in his temple pulsated like a writhing snake.

'All this emotion and pain, all this hate perhaps explains your loss of memory.' Josh stepped to his table, directing the jury's attention to the girl. He wanted them to see the bruised face. 'You hit her, didn't you, Gunderson?'

'Maybe somebody hit her,' Gunderson said. 'I don't recall.'

'If other witnesses get up on this stand and tell us you hit her, are they telling the truth?' Before Gunderson could reply, Josh said, 'You had a great deal to drink that night.'

'I suppose,' he said.

'Perhaps your memory of the events is unclear. Drunk men often forget their actions.'

'I remember she shot me. I remember that well enough.'

'Do you remember hitting her?'

Gunderson said nothing.

'Answer my question,' said Josh. 'Did you hit her?'

When Gunderson refused to answer, Judge Melrose said, 'Answer the question, Mr Lott.'

His smile gone, Gunderson cleared his throat. 'Maybe I slapped her. I was drunk. So what?'

'How much do you weigh, Mr Lott? Thirteen or fourteen stone? You stand about six foot. Now Rosa May Whitefield is no more than five four and weights eight stone. Why did a big strapping fellow like you feel compelled to strike this little lady?'

'Lady?' Gunderson laughed. 'Hell, she's a whore. She's got no right to hold out if I want her.'

'She refused you, and you hit her.'

'So?'

'And then you took her?'

'It's her business.'

'When she refused you, you beat her and took her against her will?'

'Whores are used to that kind of thing.'

'So if she refuses services, you have a right to take them on demand?' Josh said.

'She's a whore.'

'So if a feed store operator refuses to sell you a bag of oats, you have the right to beat him up and take the oats?'

Through clinched teeth, Gunderson said, 'Goddamn you, Thorn. This is more of your legal shenanigans.' He looked at the jury and said, 'Lawyer tricks.'

Judge Melrose struck the gavel. In a stern, commanding voice, he said, 'I will tell the jury when Mr Thorn is out of line, not you. So far, he seems to be asking appropriate questions.'

Gunderson turned his angry glare upon the judge, but the judge was not to be intimidated. Pointing the gavel, the judge said, 'If that fails to meet with your approval, young man, you can cool off that hot temper in the jail and continue these proceedings when you can conduct yourself accordingly.'

When Gunderson faced the front again, Josh saw much of the fight drained from his face.

Josh said, 'You paid for the services of my client?'

'I paid for my poke,' Gunderson said.

The answer drew laughs from half a dozen men.

'You paid two dollars. Is that correct?'

'That's the going rate,' he said. As if an afterthought, he

added, 'Too expensive, if you ask me.'

'But you paid your two dollars?'

'Sure, I paid my two dollars.'

'Did you also pay for Mr Smith or Mr Ash?'

'Why the hell should I do that?' Gunderson said. 'I paid my two dollars. If Smith and Ash didn't pay, that's not my fault.'

'And why did Mr Smith and Mr Ash not pay? Was it because the three of you were so busy having your way with Rosa May Whitefield that you forgot that little transaction?'

'What are you trying to say? You trying to say we raped a whore?' With the mention of the word 'rape,' a murmur arose around the room. It was a word proper gentlemen avoided using.

'You took her by force. When she said no, you beat her and took her by force. That's what happened, is it not?'

'If I bought a horse and it bucked me, then I got a right to break it.' Gunderson smiled like he had made a telling point.

'So you saw Miss Whitefield as a mare to be broken? She was only an animal, so it was quite acceptable that you brutalize her?'

'She's a whore, goddamn it!'

Judge Melrose slammed his open palm on the table. 'Considering your condition, Gunderson Lott, I have allowed you some latitude in your remarks, but I will not have cursing in this court.'

Gunderson looked contrite and was on verge of apologizing, but Josh cut him off. 'I have nothing else for this witness, Your Honor.'

Gunderson held an open palm toward the Judge. 'Look, I'm sorry—'

The judge waved him back to his seat. 'Go on, sit back down with your pa. And keep your mouth shut. I have heard about all I can stand from you.'

He turned a furious stare at Josh. 'He twisted my words all around.'

'You had your say in open court.' The judge turned to Grey. 'Marshal, this witness has ten seconds to vacate this chair. If he refuses, escort him straight to jail.'

Gunderson pushed himself to his feet. This time, caught up in his anger and frustration, he walked normally, the shifting gait gone. The jurors noticed and frowned their disapproval.

Judge Melrose said, 'Call your next witness, Marshal.'

Grey waved Jud Ash forward. Ash was a bulky man, thick in the chest and arms from hauling ore from the Bodie Mine. His face was covered in a heavy beard, which he used to hide a profusion of pox scars. A heavy white bandage covered his left hand where a piece of shot had shattered bone. Since the shooting, he had wandered from one bar to another, claiming the injury kept him from work and mooching drinks off men who would listen to his tale of woe.

When Ash dropped into the witness chair, the wood groaned like a wagon burdened with a heavy load. He stared out at the crowd, his scarred brow jutting from his head, which gave him a brutish appearance.

Judge Melrose swore him in, and Marshal Grey asked many of the same questions he'd asked Gunderson. Ash gave his answers and confirmed much of Gunderson's testimony.

After a half hour, the marshal turned the witness over to Josh.

Josh stepped close to the big man, wanting the jury to see the difference in their sizes.

'You are a big man, Mr Ash. Bigger than Gunderson Lott.' Josh pointed to Rosa May. 'Just like Gunderson Lott, you hit her. You find that acceptable behavior? Hitting a woman?'

'I don't hit women.'

'You hit Rosa May Whitefield.'

'I ain't proud of that.' Ash scratched his beard, and white flakes drifted to his flannel shirt. 'I had too much to drink. When that happens, I do bad things. Gunderson started with the girl, I went along.'

'Was that when she refused her services?'

He nodded.

'You heard Gunderson Lott. He said he paid, but you and Smith—'

Before Josh could finish his question, Ash said, 'I never meant to cheat her.' He reached in his vest pocket and pulled out two coins. He held them in his open palm so that Josh and everyone in the room could see. The silver was spit polished so they appeared as new as the day they were minted. 'I pay now.'

Laughter made its way around the room. When no one came to take the money, he placed each coin on the table where Judge Melrose sat. He turned back to Josh and crossed his huge arms over his chest.

'Then you think of yourself an honest man, Mr Ash?'

'I did wrong.' He lifted his bandaged hand to show Josh. Red and white stripes streaked the tips of his swollen fingers. 'She had no right to pull down on us with that scattergun. That hand is hurtin' all the time. When I take off the bandage, it don't look so good.'

'When Miss Whitefield came through the door with the shotgun, did she appear upset?'

'Can't say,' said Ash.

'Why not?'

'Wasn't concentrating on her face.'

'What were you concentrating on?'

'The scattergun.'

Again his comment elicited a round of laughter. Ash

found little humor in the remark. His scarred face reddened with embarrassment.

'What about after the shooting? What did Miss Whitefield do?' asked Josh.

'She just stood there holding the scattergun until Cain took it from her.'

'Did she try to run away?'

'Just stared at us with a blank look, like she was lost.'

Marshal Grey next called Cain, the owner of the Emporium. Seated in the third row, Cain pulled the bottom of his coat, straightening it so that the lines of the fine silk followed the contours of his slim body. His face, gaunt and pale almost to the point of anemia, displayed a stoic countenance, as if he had little interest in the proceedings. Josh knew this to be a façade. The little man cared a great deal for Rosa May, not only because she was the most lucrative whore in his stable but also because she represented his symbol of personal luck. His saloon and whoring businesses were on the decline, his profit margin allowing him barely to break even until Rosa May Whitefield arrived in Bodie. From that point on, his business doubled, then trebled. Every night his gaming tables were filled to capacity and every one of his whores was on her back until early morning when the last miner headed for his own bed.

Cain's reputation was an odd one. He ran a clean establishment, and his gaming appeared above board. Twice he caught his own faro dealers cheating, and he ran them out of town. Yet people distrusted him. Perhaps it was his eyes that made him appear half asleep.

'Mr Cain,' the marshal said. 'Tell us about the shooting on the night of April 6th.'

Cain focused his narrow eyes on the marshal. 'I know nothing about the shooting except what I heard in this court. The card game had finished, and I had gone back to get drinks.'

'But you heard the shooting?'

'And I saw the result.'

'Which was what?'

'Gunderson Lott and Smith were down on the floor. Ash was over in a corner holding his hand.'

'And Miss Whitefield?'

'She was at the door, holding the shotgun, the one I keep behind the bar.'

'Which you removed from her hand.'

'Yes.'

'At the moment you entered the room, did Gunderson Lott or Jud Ash or Smith have a weapon drawn?'

'None that I saw.'

Grey hooked his thumbs in his belt, casting a glance first at the judge and then Josh. He appeared to be searching for his next question when he said abruptly, 'I have no more questions for this witness.' He crossed to his table and sat down, his expression dark and brooding.

Josh found himself mystified. The information Grey drew from Cain did little more than confirm the facts that Gunderson and Ash had already introduced, facts that Josh had never contested. Then why call Cain at all? The marshal could have rested his case after Ash, but he wanted to make sure that Josh had a chance at Cain. But why?

Josh approached Cain. 'Mr Cain, how long has Miss Whitefield been in your employment?'

Cain considered the questions, using his fingers to count. 'Nigh on fourteen months.'

'In all that time, has she caused any trouble?'

Cain shook his head. 'Not once. She never pinched a poke, never hit a customer, never even uttered a curse word.'

'Never threatened a customer?' asked Josh.

'Never.'

'So she was a good employee?'

'The best,' said Cain. 'The very best.'

'Now Mr Cain, I understand that Gunderson Lott paid two dollars for the services of my client?'

'He says he paid. I never saw it.' A glint of anger flashed in the little man's eyes. 'Even if he had, the price never included beating her like he did. All the time Gunderson Lott was on top of her, he had his elbow across her throat, choking the life out of her. I feared he would kill her. When she struggled, he just pressed all the harder until she passed out.'

'You said that none of the men brandished weapons.'

'None that I saw.'

'But Gunderson Lott was using his strength to subdue Miss Whitefield. He was using his elbow to hold her down and choke her. Is that correct?'

'I thought he was going to kill her.'

Josh glanced at the jury. 'Thank you, Mr Cain. No more questions for this witness, Your honor.'

By the time Josh reseated himself, the crowd behind him was whispering among themselves. The judge struck his gavel and called for order. Josh looked over his shoulder and saw Mr Lott speak to his son. Gunderson, his head lowered, appeared contrite and submissive.

Beside Josh, Rosa May was trembling. When Josh laid his hand on hers, she refused to look at him.

'Marshal Grey, do you have any other witnesses?' Judge Melrose asked.

Without looking up, Grey shook his head. 'I guess that's it, Judge.'

'Mr Thorn, do you have any witnesses for the defense?' asked the Judge.

Josh released his hold on the girl's hand and stood.

'Yes, Your Honor.' Josh removed the timepiece from his pocket and tapped the crystal. 'It is almost noon. Perhaps we could recess until after supper. I believe the testimony will be lengthy.'

'Sounds reasonable.' The judge nodded, drawing his knuckles across his mustache. 'You jury members remember, you are not to talk of this case while you feed yourselves. Court resumes at two this afternoon. Everybody be here on time.'

Grey came to escort Rosa May back to her cell. As they passed through the swinging doors, Josh's eyes lighted on Susan Lott. She was beautiful as always. Her blonde hair was piled atop her head and crowned by a lace hat that cast her face in sensuous shadow. Her light blue dress clung to her upper body, outlining her full breasts and trim waist.

Perhaps she had just arrived, perhaps she stood there through the whole morning. Either way, her presence shocked him. He believed her sense of proper decorum would have kept her away.

Josh recalled with amazing indifference their passionate moments when their kisses and fondling threatened to engulf them. Now he was thankful she had kept a tight rein on their emotions. He wanted no part of Susan or her family. If he had compromised her, he would have felt beholden and trapped.

With an expression of disappointment, she turned from the open door and disappeared.

8

Entering his office, Josh discovered Sammy Chung and Sing Tong waiting for him. Sing Tong, his face passive and disinterested, stood beside the door. Sammy stayed by the window, watching the street below. As Josh closed the door, Sammy rose and gave a slight bow.

'You have done your best, my friend. That was all I asked.'

'The trial is not over,' said Josh. 'I have witnesses to call this afternoon.'

'No doubt that includes Miss Whitefield.' Sammy turned again to the window to watch the street. 'It would be best if you do not.'

Josh tossed his hat on the desk. 'Does she know too many details of your business? Is that why you fear her testimony?'

'You believe I would betray this woman to save my business interests some embarrassment? Even if the good people of Bodie closed down one of my establishments, it would reopen within the week.'

'Her story is important. If I can just get one man on that jury to understand what the woman has gone through. . . .'

Outside the wind blew from the west, threatening more rain. Josh stepped to the woodpile, drew out two logs, and stuffed them in the stove. He closed the grate. Coals left from the morning caught the dry wood and a blaze erupted. Josh dropped in the chair behind his desk.

Sammy said, 'Many women of her profession have such stories. Hers is not unusual and not likely to persuade the jury.' Sammy made a movement with his right hand as if he were shooing away a fly. 'Please understand first that Miss Whitefield never confided in me about any part of her life. I am not the kind of person a woman like Miss Whitefield would confide in. No, she told Mai Ling, who in turn, told me.'

'You never thought I could win this case, did you, Sammy?' Josh said.

'I knew from the first that the community would align against you, and Miss Whitefield would be found guilty.'

'Then why did you push me to represent her?'

Sammy stroked his chin as he appraised Josh. 'She needed a man in whom she could trust, in whom she could believe. There have been so few in her young life.'

After Sammy left, Josh opened the Bible at random, his finger alighting on Genesis 19, and he read the story of Lot and his daughters. By the time he finished, he had sunk deeper into depression. No answers there. Daughters who got their father drunk and slept with him in order to preserve his seed offered little in the way of hope. He shoved the book in the top drawer of the desk.

He pulled his pocket watch from his vest and stared at the moving second hand. The trial was due to resume in less than twenty minutes. He was tired, and he would have loved to have slept for an hour or so and forget about the future. Instead, he pushed himself to his feet and left the office.

At the bottom of the stairs, he was met by Pastor Warrington. An awkward pause followed before the pastor cleared his throat and spoke. 'Ah, Joshua, good to see you. Missed you at services yesterday.'

'I had to prepare for the trial.'

Josh tried to move past, but Warrington touched him on

the arm. 'I have prayed for God to give you guidance.' Josh pulled his arm free, and Warrington said, 'Remember what Paul said to the Ephesians. "Take unto you the whole armor of God that ye may be able to withstand in the evil day." You must follow the righteous path, my son.'

'You know, just before we ran into each other, I was reading the Bible,' Josh said. 'The story of Lot and his daughters.'

The reverend frowned. 'A disturbing story.'

'At one spot Lot is willing to give his virgin daughters to the mob from Sodom. Later Lot planted his seed in his daughters. Each daughter bore him a child.'

'The daughters clouded the mind of the old man with liquor.' The pastor's face turned hard and stern as if he were giving a lecture. 'God saved Lot and his family only because Abraham asked a favor from God. But Lot was a weak man and little better than his fellow Sodomites. A wicked story. Truly wicked.'

'And the lesson in the story?' asked Josh.

'Lot followed the word of God, and thus he was spared,' said the pastor.

Pointing, Josh drew the attention of Reverend Warrington to the wall of the building where ants scurried up and down in a moving line. One ant had strayed. 'See that ant. Perhaps he knows or senses that hovering above him is something larger, something infinitely more intelligent.'

The pastor narrowed his eyes as if he were unsure of direction of the conversation.

'I am God to that ant. I hold the power of life and death.' With a quick jab, he crushed the insect with the heel of his hand. 'So much for a caring God.'

The other ants continued their steady stream, unaffected by the death of their comrade.

'Good day, Pastor.' Josh stepped around the man.

Reverend Warrington called after him. 'She is a lost soul doomed to everlasting fire. You cannot save her, Joshua. No one can.'

Josh ignored the man and continued on to the jail. When he entered the office, he found Grey behind the desk bent over a stack of wanted posters. Josh continued to the cells.

Her back against the cold stone, Rosa May sat on the bunk, a blanket thrown across her shoulders. Her smile was warm and grateful, but she was a woman on the emotional edge. He saw it in her eyes. He understood then that Sammy was right. Putting her on the stand would accomplish nothing. If he were going to win this case, it must be without her testimony.

She rose from the cot and came to him. Wordless, she leaned forward, and he slipped one arm through the bars and around her shoulders. He had never before touched a whore in so intimate a fashion, but truth be told, he had ceased to think of her in that way. All the men she had serviced, all her vile, licentious deeds meant little now. She was just a lost, fragile girl in need of kindness.

'I won't let them hurt you. I promise.'

With sudden fury she pushed him away. 'They will find me guilty, and they will hang me. You know it, I know it. There can be no other way.'

'Have I promised anything I failed to deliver?'

'I have no chance. None. I knew that the moment I pulled the trigger. What happens next can only be a blessed relief.' She sat back on the cot and placed her back against the cold stone. 'I appreciate all you've done, but now it ends.'

'Listen to me, damn it! Whatever happens, I will not let them hurt you. I mean it. And never again question my word. I am not a liar, and I am not one to give false hope.'

Her dark eyes held his, and his stomach fluttered with desire. He wanted to kiss her, to crush his lips against hers.

'Whatever happens in court, you are not to despair,' Josh said. 'If the verdict goes against us, it means nothing. There are other alternatives.'

'You plan to appeal my case.' She smiled as a mother might smile to a small child.

In a mining town such as Bodie, courts of appeal did not exist. If this were San Francisco or Sacramento, it might be different, but an unincorporated mining community operated on its own law. Once a jury made up its mind, it carried out justice swiftly and conclusively. Then, as if divining his intentions, she said, 'You are planning a foolish thing.'

'I am planning nothing except making this charge against you go away.'

When he returned to the front office, Josh stopped before Grey. The lanky marshal kept his eyes focused on the wanted posters. Josh said, 'Today when you called Cain to the stand, you gave me an opening.'

Grey lifted his head, an angry scowl twisting his face. 'If you spread that around, so help me God—'

'I intend to tell no one. I only want to know why.'

His hands flat against the desk, Grey pushed his chair back and stood. 'I did nothing of the sort. That is crazy talk.'

'Regardless of your motives, I appreciate the chance. You're a decent man, Marshal, a fair man.'

Josh was walking out the door when Grey said, 'Good luck, Thorn.'

Half an hour later, Josh was back in the courtroom with Rosa May seated beside him.

Judge Melrose banged the gavel for the trial to resume, and the saloon grew quiet.

'Call your first witness, Mr Thorn,' the judge ordered.

Josh stood. 'Judge, I call Marshal Grey to the stand.'

Judge Melrose waved the marshal forward to the witness chair. Grey came around the table and settled himself where the judge swore him in. He fidgeted in the chair and glowered at Josh.

Josh said, 'You heard Mr Cain testify earlier of Miss Whitefield's conduct. Has she ever given you problems as a law officer, other than this current situation?'

'No.' Grey glanced beyond Josh to Mr Lott and his son who had reclaimed their seats. 'This was the first and only time.'

'Do you get many complaints about women in her profession?'

'Every day.'

'My client has been here for fourteen months, and you've not received one complaint against her. Would you say that's unusual?' Josh asked.

'Yes.'

Josh rested his case. He might have called other witnesses to the girl's character such as Sammy Chung or Mai Lin or Mother Mapes, but he doubted their words would have found sympathy with the jurors. The jurors were white men, and most white men in Bodie took little stock in the word of anyone of color.

'Let us have your summations.' Judge Melrose waved his gavel at Josh.

Standing before the jury, Josh searched the face of each man, hoping to find one among them who appeared sympathetic to his cause. He knew each well enough to greet if they passed on the street, and yet here they were, strangers who stared back with hard faces. If he read anything in them, he read defeat. Still, a face is not a heart, and inside one of these men might beat the barest spark of compassion. Perhaps one or more had exchanged money for Rosa May's services, and if so, might feel some connection.

He began his summation by reiterating the events of the night of April 6th, concentrating on the actions of Gunderson, Smith and Jud Ash. He portrayed them as drunken, cruel men who took a woman against her will and brutalized her in the process.

'As you will recall, Jud Ash himself told you he was sorry, that he knew he had done a bad thing. This is a man we can respect, a man who has the courage to admit that he's done a morally reprehensible act. Did we hear any such confession from Gunderson Lott? No, we did not. And why? Because he feels he has done no wrong. As he said himself, you pay for a mare, and it's your right to break her. Is that what we believe here in Bodie? That women are no better than horses? I hope and pray that is not so.

'The question that confronts us, gentlemen, is not whether Rosa May Whitefield shot and killed Smith and wounded Gunderson Lott and Jud Ash. Those are indisputable facts. Rather, the question you must decide is: Did the men that night push this girl beyond all endurance? Did her violation justify her actions? Do the actions of Gunderson Lott and the others reflect the moral standing of this community? My God, I hope not!

'I ask you to bring in the only fair verdict. Dismiss the charges against Rosa May Whitefield and send a message to men who lay their hands on women that such behavior is unacceptable.'

When Josh seated himself, Grey approached the jury. 'I don't have much to say, and I certainly can't say it as well as Mr Thorn. The facts are laid out before you. Rosa May Whitefield used a scattergun to shoot and kill this fellow Smith. In that attack, she also wounded Gunderson Lott and Jud Ash. One man dead, two injured. No one threatened her, no one had a weapon drawn. This was not self-defense. Now Mr Thorn reminds you of all the indignities Miss

Whitefield suffered, but you just keep reminding yourself that she killed a man.' He looked directly at Josh and the girl. 'She meant to kill all three. There's only one verdict you can reach. I see no other.'

The jury retired to a back room. They were gone less than ten minutes before they returned with a verdict of guilty. Judge Melrose sentenced Rosa May Whitefield to be hanged by the neck until she was dead, the sentence to be carried out at noon the following day at the Bodie Livery and Feed where the hoist jutted out over the street.

9

They rounded the top of the hill where the trail curved down into the bowl-shaped valley. Before them lay Bodie. High atop the southern bluff, watching over the town like a benevolent god, stood the Bodie Mine. Even from here, Virgil heard the metal lifts bringing the raw rock up from the earth and the machinery grinding it into dust so that the water systems could filter out the gold. For the most part, the city was all wooden structures, many of them little more than shacks. Heaps of trash and discarded machinery lay in piles behind buildings, and a few patches of snow had turned brown with dirt and grime. Taken as a whole, Bodie was unimpressive, especially for a community from which flowed so much wealth.

They passed the cemetery where many of the headstones sat at oblique angles, left that way by the heavy winter snows, and their very presence seemed a sign to Virgil that his odyssey neared its end. For three years he had searched for the killer of his brother, and now the man was there among those buildings. Virgil feared neither Thorn nor death itself, but he did fear Thorn might have fled from here, too. If that proved to be the case, his disappointment would be almost too much to bear.

Earlier that morning when they had ridden out of Bridgeport, they had worn their heavy coats. As the day warmed, they stripped down to their shirts. Now, unimpeded, Virgil rested the heel of his hand on the butt of his .44 and thought of Thorn.

Harkness noticed the gesture. 'I thought you hired me to do the job.'

Virgil placed both hands back on the reins. 'Whether you or I pull the trigger, you get paid just the same.'

'As long as I ain't cheated out of my bounty.' Harkness spit, and a dark wad of tobacco juice splattered in the dirt.

They rode up Main Street. Piano music from half a dozen saloons blended into one discordant sound. Men lined both sides of the street and shouted obscenities and jokes. Painted women moved among the men, attempting to entice them to the shacks out back.

'A festive atmosphere. Is the town always like this?' asked Virgil.

'More lively than usual,' Harkness said.

They drew up before the Livery and Feed and dismounted. A young boy no more than thirteen or fourteen came to take their mounts. His shirt was frayed around the collar and cuffs. When he smiled, he showed a pair of buck teeth. Virgil handed him a silver dollar and asked, 'Something special going on today?'

The boy nodded. 'We just had a whiz bang trial. A whore killed a man, and tomorrow, right here, right from our very own hoist, we're going to—' Using the reins, he dangled them beside his neck and tilted his head to simulate a hanging.

'You know a Joshua Thorn?' asked Virgil.

'Sure as heck. I guess just about everybody in town knows him. He was the whore's lawyer.'

'And where can I find him?' asked Virgil.

'That I can't rightly say. You might try the Emporium. That's where they held the trial. He might still be there.'

Virgil gave the boy an extra half dime. Staring at the coin, the boy led the horses and mule into the stable.

Harkness glanced up at the hoist. 'I seen men dangling from there, but never a woman. That's going to be something to see.'

'Once we finish the business at hand, you are welcome to stay and watch. Otherwise, keep your mind on the task.'

'Then let's find this Thorn and get it over with.' Harkness took the .44 from his holster and checked the rounds.

When they entered the Emporium, they found the bar packed two deep and every chair at the gaming tables filled. Behind the bar, a dozen waiters ran back and forth pouring drinks. A few women, their faces heavy with rouge, milled among the men, trying to wrangle drinks and money.

With his hand on his pistol, Virgil searched the room for Thorn. He believed he would recognize the man, even though the years might have changed him. There was also the chance that Thorn had deliberately altered his appearance. Perhaps he had grown a beard or put on weight.

'Well?' asked Harkness.

'He is not here.'

From out of the crowd, a voice roared, 'Bib! Bib Harkness!' A large man separated himself from the bar and stepped forward. 'So you came back after all.'

Harkness tensed. 'You ain't wearing your star.'

'And I ain't looking for trouble neither,' said Lauter. 'Hell, the trouble you had weren't with me. It was with Grey.'

'You were his deputy.' A bitter tone infected Harkness' voice.

'And he fired me for no reason at all. I never had anything to do with what happened. Hell, you was gone before I had a chance to say so long.' With his hand, he motioned toward the bar. 'Let me buy you a drink.' He cast a glance at Virgil. 'Hell, I'll stand one for your friend, too.'

Harkness followed Lauter who pushed his way to the bar. Harkness was such a short man that Lauter dwarfed him, but Virgil had no doubt who feared whom.

At the bar Lauter ordered three whiskies. While they waited, Harkness studied the big man's face full of deep bruises around the eyes and jaw. His lip was split, which would leave a nasty scar.

'Somebody gave you a working over,' said Harkness.

'The little bastard caught me unawares. His name is Thorn, and—'

'Joshua Thorn?' asked Virgil.

Lauter turned to face Virgil. 'You a friend of his?' The question carried an implied threat.

Harkness said, 'Settle down, big man. Mr Perry is no friend of Thorn, though him and me have come a long distance to pay him a visit.'

Lauter smiled. 'When you visit people, Bib, they often wind up in a wooden box.'

'Where is Thorn?' Virgil asked.

' 'Bout an hour ago I saw him heading toward his office. Ain't seen him since.'

'And the marshal? Where is he?' asked Harkness.

'In his office guarding the little whore that we're going to hang tomorrow.' The bartender brought the drinks, and Lauter lifted the glass in a toast. 'Welcome back, Bib.'

Harkness held up the glass and inspected the color of the whiskey before he drank.

'Suppose something happened to Grey. Who would be marshal then?'

Lauter shrugged. 'He ain't got a deputy. Guess there would be nobody.'

With a smile, Harkness sipped the whiskey. 'How would you like the job?'

'Grey ain't likely to quit,' said Lauter.

'Maybe he ain't got a choice.'

'In that case, somebody would have to be marshal.'

'My sentiments favor you,' said Harkness.

In a low, firm voice, Virgil said, 'I did not hire you to settle a personal grudge, Mr Harkness.'

Harkness grunted. 'You think Marshal Grey is just going to let you and me walk up to Thorn and kill him? Grey ain't that kind of peace officer. He will put a stop to us if we don't put a stop to him first.'

Virgil said, 'And what happens if Marshal Grey stops you first, Mr Harkness?'

'Won't happen,' said Harkness.

'Apparently he ran you out of here once before.'

Harkness narrowed his eyes and spit, the brown juice splattering in the sawdust covered floor. 'He had a gun in my ribs before I knew what was happening. He ain't sneaking up on me again.'

'I fear you jeopardize our plans,' said Virgil.

'I ain't jeopardizing nothing. In plain fact, I aim to make sure nothing gets in the way.' Harkness laid the half empty glass on the bar. 'I need a clear head for what I have to do.'

Harkness pushed his way through the boisterous crowd with Lauter and Virgil following. Directly across the street lay the jail. Harkness paused to survey the structure. Virgil said, 'I will take no part in this enterprise.'

'I have no need of your help.' With his thumb, Harkness poked Lauter in the chest. 'However, you will assist me.'

Fear pinched Lauter's eyes.

Harkness said, 'The gunplay is mine. You call Grey outside. Get him through the door. I will see to the rest.' When Lauter failed to acquiesce, Harkness said, 'You get something out of this, but not for nothing. Understand?'

Harkness crossed the street at an oblique angle, taking each step carefully to avoid slipping in the mud. He placed himself to the right of the door near the edge of the building. With a wave, he signaled Lauter who hung back, fearing to take that first step. In the middle of the street, Lauter would present an easy target. But when Harkness gestured a second time, Lauter gathered his courage and stepped off the walk, his boots sinking to his ankles as he plowed through the mud. He walked like a man in a trance, his shoulders rolling forward, oblivious to events and people around him. Twice riders on horses had to veer to keep from trampling him.

Virgil positioned himself behind a wagon from where he could see the action. All along the walk, men passed without the slightest idea what was about to take place. The saloons continued to emit their revelry. Gruff voices mixed with piano music and the laughter of women. From further up the street, a caravan of three wagons moved down from the mine, the mules leaning into the traces.

Then, all these distractions ceased to exist when Lauter called out, 'Marshal Grey. Come on out here?' Lauter did his best to keep his voice level, but on 'here', it went high. When the door failed to open right away, Lauter called out again, 'Grey.'

The door opened, and the marshal stepped out. Bareheaded, his long yellow hair hung to his shoulders. His dark coat dropped below his waist, but he had pulled the tail back to give his hands a clear path to his pistols. To Virgil he was an imposing figure, but what struck him was the look in the man's eye. It was cold and deadly, and Virgil thought him the most dangerous man he had ever seen.

'What the hell do you want, Lauter?' Grey asked.

In a quivering voice, Lauter said, 'Not me.'

Sensing danger, Grey whirled, drawing his right pistol. He was too late. Harkness fired, the big .44 jumping with the recoil. All along the walk, men leapt for cover, and Lauter dove headlong into the street, throwing his hands over his head and burying his face in the mud.

The force of the blast threw the marshal against the door frame. Using the palm of his left hand, Harkness fanned the hammer, firing off two more shots in quick succession. Grey fell, his tall body spread along the walk where gun smoke swirled over him like ground fog.

The street, which had grown quiet and still, came to life as men picked themselves up or stepped from cover. Virgil went to Lauter who stood wiping his face with his sleeve.

Grey groaned, and Lauter said, 'He's still alive, Bib.'

Harkness flashed a wry smile. 'He's dead. He just don't know it yet.'

By now, a crowd of men had gathered around the fallen Grey. Harkness faced them.

'Anyone need to dispute what happened here?'

The crowd remained silent. These were miners and store-keepers whose proficiency with weapons was modest at best. Each man realized that a challenge would result in the same fate as Grey.

Harkness said, 'This town needs a new lawman.' Bending, he plucked the star from Grey's vest. When he straightened, he laid a hand on Lauter's shoulder. 'I nominate Lauter.'

No one offered an objection.

10

Five minutes before three, Josh entered the Bodie Bank where he informed the manager he wished to withdraw $700 to purchase two claims across the Nevada line. This was a lie, of course. He left over one hundred in his account to make the withdrawal appear more legitimate. The manager gave him $600 in paper and a hundred in twenty dollar gold pieces.

His next stop was the house of Sammy Chung. Mai Lin led him into the living room and left Josh alone with Sammy.

'I need your help,' said Josh.

'For what, my friend? A foolish gesture?' Sammy said.

'I will do what I have to with or without your help, Sammy. But since it was you who got me into this, I think you owe me.'

Sammy stroked his chin. 'Yes, you will do this thing, regardless of my actions.' He called out in Chinese, and Sing Tong entered the room. Sammy spoke rapidly, and when he finished, the diminutive bodyguard bowed and exited. Sammy said, 'I need at least two hours.'

Josh returned to his room where he stuffed his saddle bags with clothing and shells for his pistol and rifle. Fully clothed, he dropped on the bed and closed his eyes, intending to sleep until it was time to see Sammy. Sleep proved elusive.

Finally, he sat on the side of the bed, removed the pistol from his holster. It was a Colt .44, the most popular handgun among the men of Bodie, and it came in two barrel lengths, the longer seven and a half inches and the shorter five and a half inches. Those who considered themselves fast draw artists chose the shorter length, but Josh preferred the longer barrel because the extra weight gave it stability. He was a good shot but not particularly fast. A hundred men in Bodie were faster.

Josh checked the rounds, removing each cartridge, dropping it back into the chamber. Six chambers, six rounds.

Standing, he slipped the gun belt around his waist, and hefting his rifle and saddle bags, left the room.

When he came through the door, Sammy lifted an eyebrow. 'A bit early, my friend. It has been barely an hour.'

'I would rather stay here,' Josh said.

'It is strange to hear a white man say he would rather stay in my house than his own dwelling.' He motioned Josh to a cushioned seat. 'Of course. It may be a while before we have such a chance again.'

Josh laid his gear beside the chair. 'When I leave Bodie, I am gone for good, Sammy.'

'Do not be so certain, Joshua. Life has its strange little twists and turns.' Sammy seated himself, folding his arms inside his sleeves. 'We may meet again. I hope so. You have proven a worthy friend. I am sad at your going.'

'My days are finished here. Those who run this town, Lott and the others, will see to that.'

A pained expression deepened the lines around Sammy's mouth and eyes. 'I must confess, I misjudged this whole situation. I believed you would offer a spirited defense, the girl would lose, and that would be the end of it. I never sensed the passion you harbored for Miss Whitefield. A major miscalculation on my part.'

Josh laughed. 'I surprised you for once. I thought such a thing impossible.'

'I do apologize, Joshua.' Sammy lowered his head as if ashamed.

'No regrets, Sammy. I will play my hand to the finish. Maybe my luck has run out, maybe not. We'll see.'

Sing Tong entered and spoke a few words in Chinese. Sammy rose and said, 'Please excuse me.' He followed his protégé out of the room.

Far away on Main Street, Josh heard a pistol bark followed by two more in rapid succession. He wondered idly who had gotten himself killed this time, and that led to the most depressing thought of all. He saw himself lying in the mud of Main Street, his life's blood draining away. If that came to pass, then what had brought him to such an inglorious end? The girl surely was at the center of all that had happened. Her face haunted his every waking hour. But he also saw that more than just a pretty face had brought him to this cross-roads. His own sense of justice had also been the culprit.

Sammy returned, this time holding a map. Following close behind came a tall Paiute whose dark skin showed deep wrinkles around his mouth and eyes. He wore a leather shirt and breeches. A brown kerchief circled his neck, another his forehead. A strip of rawhide held together his long hair. From the moment the man entered the room, Josh caught the smell of desert, horses and sweat.

The main body of Paiutes lived southeast of Bodie in the Panamint Valley, but individually they ranged the mountains from Death Valley to the Sierras. In the summer and early fall, a contingent of Paiutes, perhaps as many as a hundred, took up residence just outside of town. Many of the men wore cast-off hats or clothes of white people, and the women wore blankets and hung wicker cradles on their backs in which they carried their children. Among the socially-conscious whites of Bodie, the Paiutes were even below the Chinese, but they seldom caused any trouble, although when a chicken or dog went missing, people were fond of blaming them.

Most Paiutes stood below five six or seven, but at almost six feet, this man towered over most of his people.

Sammy said, 'Joshua Thorn, allow me to introduce Mr Raven.'

'Raven?' Josh said.

'A misnomer, but accurate,' the man said, his voice the deepest bass Josh had ever heard. 'In my language, I am called Black Bird That Disappears in the Night. For simplicity's sake, Raven will do quite nicely.'

'Your English is impeccable.' Josh held out his hand, and without hesitation, Raven stepped forward and took it. 'I defended a fellow tribesman of yours,' Josh said. 'His name was Sand, I believe. He was charged with horse stealing. You stood just outside the back door, and every once in a while, you would look in.'

'Sand was my brother.'

'Your brother?' As Josh remembered, they looked nothing alike. Sand was smaller with a much lighter complexion.

'My father was a slave who came West to escape.' Raven closed his arms over his chest. His face had turned to stone. 'He died before I was born. Our mother, who was Paiute, remarried one of her own tribe.'

'As I am sure you will remember, Joshua,' Sammy said, 'you had the charges against Mr Sand dismissed.'

'It was an easy case. Lauter brought charges without substance. The judge rightly threw the case out of court.'

'As usual you did a thorough job,' said Sammy. 'And Mr Raven would like to thank you personally.'

'And how is your brother?' Josh asked.

Raven's brows came together, and the fury in his eyes was palpable. The Indian pulled the kerchief away from his neck and exposed a bright red scar that ran lengthwise across his neck.

Sammy said, 'Soon after the trial, Mr Lauter and a group of his companions caught Mr Sand and Mr Raven alone in the hills. They killed Mr Sand and left Mr Raven for dead. He managed to cross ten miles of mountains to reach my house and sanctuary. He hovered near death for days, but human beings have a tenacity for life. As you see, Mr Raven has fully recovered. And now, Mr Raven has agreed to help.'

Sammy unrolled the map on the table, placing weights on each end to keep it open. The map was of the White and Sierras Mountains and the valley that separated them, running from Bridgeport in the north to Lone Pine in the south, from Death Valley in the east to the San Joaquin Valley in the west. With his index finger, Sammy traced a path that led from Bodie down the mountains to Mono Lake and beyond. He followed the valley until it began a long, steep descent. Here he left the valley and followed a canyon into the Sierras that led up through a series of lakes.

'These are the Mammoth Lakes,' he said. 'If you can reach these and cross over Granite Pass to Convict Lake, you will be safe. The pass will be full of snow, and for perhaps a quarter mile, the terrain will be too rugged for horses. Pursuit will follow. When you abandon your horses, they will be sure that you are trapped. They will leave their mounts and follow on foot. Once you navigate the pass, fresh horses will be waiting on the other side. Mr Raven has already sent another of his cousins to Convict Lake to acquire horses and meet you at the far end of Granite Pass. Once you are on fresh mounts and headed down the mountain, you will have evaded pursuit.'

Josh smiled. 'A splendid plan, Sammy.'

The door opened, and Sing Tong entered. He spoke to Sammy, and Sammy said, 'Two strangers have arrived in town. Apparently, they are seeking you, Joshua.'

'Me?'

'One carries the name of Harkness.'

'I know no one by that name,' said Josh.

'The other calls himself Virgil Perry,' said Sammy.

'Damn!' Josh slammed a fist against the table.

'I see that name holds meaning.' Sammy raised an inquisitive eyebrow.

'My past has caught up with me,' said Josh.

'I regret to say there is more,' said Sammy. 'This Mr Harkness, who I now believe to be a hired assassin, has shot Marshal Grey.'

'Is he dead?' Josh asked.

'He was carried to the Lott's house where the doctor was called. I am afraid he is severely injured. This is too bad. He is a stern man but fair. When he arrested my people, he never mistreated them as others have done. And Mr Lauter has assumed the role of marshal. And I believe that these men, Harkness and Lauter, mean you harm.'

The thought of Grey out of the way should have made Josh feel easier. The marshal was a dangerous man, and the thought of dealing with him had put a pall over the whole enterprise.

Josh swept up his rifle and saddle bags. 'Sooner or later, they will come here, Sammy. They may be heading here right this minute.'

Sammy glanced at Raven who nodded. 'Mr Raven and I have discussed the situation. We both feel you should make your move early in the morning, perhaps around three, when the streets are less crowded. Mr Raven and I have taken the liberty to draw up a plan of action, one designed to get you and Miss Whitefield safely out of town. Mr Raven will explain.'

Josh listened carefully. It was a simple plan based on deception. If it worked, Josh, Rosa May, and Raven would be miles away before anyone knew they were gone.

'For the present, you will go with Sing Tong,' Sammy said. 'I suggest you get some rest, my friend. You will need it for the trials ahead.'

Sing Tong escorted Josh through the house where heavy curtains hugged the windows and dark shadows haunted every corner. Alien artwork stood on pedestals and lined the walls. They exited a rear door that led to a street lined with shacks. Here Chinese women hung out washing or watched their children play or cooked over open stoves. Josh and Sing Tong also passed a few men dressed in coolie outfits and wearing pigtails that hung down their backs. Not one took notice.

They arrived at another structure where Sing Tong stepped into the dark interior. Once inside, Josh smelled the sweet incense that attempted to cover the raw, pungent odor of opium. When the door closed, he stood very still, allowing his eyes to adjust.

Sing Tong said, 'Mr Chung has awarded you great honor. You are first white man to enter here. Now, please follow. I take you to room where you wait.'

They entered a large formal room where in one corner a figure of Buddha sat on a raised dais. Candles and incense burned in trays around its base, and a cloud hung in the middle of the room, highlighted by the flickering flames. A half dozen old men, their thin beards hanging to their breastbones, sat cross-legged on rugs and pillows, their lips pursed around wooden tips attached to tubes that in turn were attached to glass bowls filled with water. Occasionally one of the old men would inhale, holding the smoke in his lungs before expelling it. In a tier of beds against the far wall, another group of old men slept soundly, lost in manufactured dreams.

Stepping behind the Buddha, Sing Tong led Josh to a door, which opened into a small enclave. A bed was pressed up against one corner and next to it, a table and chair. The tiny room had no window, but a skylight allowed the sun to filter through.

Once Sing Tong left, Josh dropped his saddle-bags and rifle beside the bed. Without removing his boots, he lay down. Although he was less than five foot nine, his feet hung over the end. Shifting his weight, he found a comfortable spot and slipped his hat over his eyes and told himself to relax.

A light rapping at the door awakened him. The room was a black cave, and Josh was momentarily disoriented. Only when he saw the muted stars through the skylight did he remember where he was. He threw his legs over the side of the bed.

The door opened, and Mai Lin entered carrying a tray, which she laid on the table. She lit a lamp, turning the wick low so that the corners of the small room remained buried in deep shadows.

Josh's stomach grumbled, and he moved to the table. The bowl was filled with noodles, vegetables and meat.

Mai Lin said, 'Sing Tong come soon.'

'I am ready,' Josh said.

'Tonight, I offer prayers for you and my friend, Miss Whitefield.'

Josh looked into her face, beautifully sculptured by the shadows, and he saw there a combination of anguish and fear.

'Thank you,' he said, and she was gone, the door closing silently behind her.

He wondered then to whose god she prayed, and he realized it must be her own, the stone figure that rested in the room outside his door. With that thought came a sudden sense of irony. Here he was, a Christian man who believed in a Christian god, seeking refuge in a place of idols. Those who called themselves Christians were the ones out to crucify the girl while the heathens – the Chinese and Paiutes – were the only ones willing to help her.

After he ate, he sat there an hour, perhaps longer, before the door again opened and Sing Tong entered, gesturing for him to follow. Carrying his rifle and saddle-bags, Josh stepped into the outer room. Sammy Chung stood beside the statue of Buddha, and Josh thought it odd that both Buddha and Sammy had little bellies that rolled out against their robes. However, Sammy stood taller than his god-like counterpart.

The old men who inhabited this room earlier were gone, but when he spoke, Sammy whispered as if he feared to be overheard. 'Just as you surmised, your enemies came to my house looking for you. For the moment, they believe you have fled for Bridgeport. By morning, they will know differently. We must hurry now.' Sammy slid his hand from his sleeve and held it out to Josh. 'I am going to miss you, my friend. You added character to a town that has little.'

Josh took his hand and held it firmly.

Outside the night had grown chilly. Josh slipped on his coat before he followed Sing Tong along King Street until it intersected Main Street. There, deep in shadows, the two men found Raven, who took the saddle-bags and rifle from Josh.

Sing Tong said, 'Mr Raven wait beside jail with horses. We must be swift.'

Josh pushed the coat away from the pistol and stepped out of the protection of the shadows. He rounded Main Street and headed for the jail. Across the way in the Emporium, a dozen customers remained at the bar with their drinks, but the lamps over the tables and roulette wheel were extinguished. Keeping to the shadows, Josh worked his way along the front of the jail.

The door was a dark slab, and Josh gave a push, swinging it inward. The outer office was so black that he had to wait until his eyes adjusted. Fighting back his fear, he crossed the room, pausing only long enough to pluck the keys from their resting place on the wall. As he pushed open the door to the cells, a voice said, 'Hold it right there, Sky Pilot.'

Slowly Josh turned to face the dark phantom outlined by the light from the saloon.

'Your friend Sammy Chung sold you out.' Lauter laughed. 'Made a deal with me. I paid him a hundred dollars, and when I turn you over to Virgil Perry, he'll pay me $500 more. Nice little profit, huh?'

Lauter laughed again, but before the laugh died, his head flew back, and he grunted. As Lauter fell, Sing Tong hit him again, the heel of his hand thudding into the thick neck with a solid snap. Lauter's face bounced off the floor.

When Josh entered the cell area, he heard the swish of a dress as Rosa May came to the bars.

'You should not have come,' she said.

He shoved the key in the lock and turned it, the metal clanging against metal.

As she stepped from the cell, the light from outside exposed a fresh bruise on the left side her face just below the eye.

'Lauter?' he asked.

'It doesn't matter.'

'Come on. We best be on the move.'

'Wait.' She dashed back into the cell, and a moment later, re-emerged carrying the Shakespeare volume.

In the outer office, he stopped beside Lauter, who lay motionless. For a brief instant, he considered putting a bullet in the man, but to do so would bring the town down on their heads. Instead, he delivered a kick that cracked against the man's face. With that, Josh and the girl fled into the black night.

11

At five the next afternoon, a miner dropped into the Emporium, and in the middle of a beer, remarked off-handedly that he had passed that lawyer fellow on the trail riding fast for Bridgeport. Sitting at a table less than five feet away, Virgil heard the remark. The miner also mentioned that Thorn's mount appeared to have a limp, possibly a stone bruise on the left rear hoof. That gave Virgil all the hope he needed. If he and Harkness rode all night, they would overtake Thorn before Bridgeport.

The sun set behind the western mountains, and the trail darkened until it was only an outline in the night. This brought grumbles from Harkness, who complained about riding at night on a trail that descended at such a steep angle.

'I fear one of us is likely to break his neck,' he said.

They passed no one until just past eight when they encountered two freighters seated beside their wagon, a bright fire lighting their camp. When the freighters heard the horses, they reached for their rifles.

Harkness hailed them. 'Emmett Lane. I see you there. This is Bib Harkness. Just me and my companion.'

The thicker of the two men said, 'Come in slow, Bib.'

Virgil could not blame these men for their caution. Stories abounded of bandits and road agents who would rob you for your boots. Travelers who were careless lost their lives, and it behooved men to be wary of strangers. Slowly Virgil and Harkness guided their mounts into the ring of light, but neither man made a move to dismount. The freighters had yet to make an offer.

'Haven't seen you around for a while, Bib.' The thick man named Emmett showed a mouth full of missing teeth. 'You travel late.'

'We are looking for a man you passed on the road. He was riding a nag with a limp. His name is Thorn,' said Harkness.

'You talking 'bout the lawyer? The one from Bodie?'

'How long ago did he pass?' asked Harkness.

The freighter looked questioningly at his companion. 'He ain't come this way tonight.'

In a thin high voice, the other man said, 'You two is the first we seen since the sun set. We prefer it that way, to tell the truth.'

'Thank you, gentlemen.' Virgil whirled his horse back in the direction of Bodie.

When Harkness caught up to him, Virgil said, 'We have been led astray, Mr Harkness. Joshua Thorn is still in Bodie. He would not leave the woman. He will make a move to get her out.' With his right hand, Virgil slapped his leg as if it were to blame for his shortsightedness.

'He'd do that for a whore?' Harkness asked.

'Joshua Thorn is a fool for a woman in trouble,' said Virgil.

'Bodie is uphill all the way, and our horses are dragging. I doubt that we will make it much before three in the morning,' said Harkness. 'By now, he is fled in the opposite direction.'

The little gunman obviously wanted to stop and camp for the night. Virgil understood. He, too, was saddle weary.

'Lauter won't let anybody get to the girl,' Harkness said.

'Your friend seems none too smart.' Virgil touched his mount with his spurs, urging him on. 'I place little faith in his ability to hold out against Thorn.'

'We must sleep sometime,' Harkness shouted after him, and then he, too, spurred his horse forward.

By the time they reached Bodie, it was near three in the morning. Both men were exhausted, and the horses were blowing heavily, the sweat thick on their withers. Never in his life had Virgil pushed animals to such extremes, and he hoped they had not ruined them. Still, if he caught Thorn, the price was worth such sacrifices.

Glancing at Harkness, Virgil saw that the man rode slumped in the saddle, either asleep or close to it. On the other hand, Virgil was alert, despite his exhaustion. The town was quiet. If Thorn had managed to break the girl out of jail, he had done so without raising a row. He rode straight for the jail. If Thorn had yet to make his move, Virgil would wait for him. Sooner or later, Thorn would come.

And then, out of the night, a hundred feet in front of him, the jail door opened and two figures emerged. Virgil didn't have to see them to understand. He reached for his pistol and dug his spurs into his mount. The mount screamed its displeasure and jumped forward. Virgil fired. Beside him, Harkness came instantly awake, but his horse, frightened by the gunshot, reared back, tossing Harkness into the air.

Virgil snapped off another shot that whined away in the darkness.

Thorn pushed the girl behind him, drew his pistol and fired. Virgil heard the bullet strike the chest of the horse, and suddenly he was flying into black space. He landed in the muddy street, skidding face down. A great weight slammed into him, knocking him senseless. When he tried to move, only his left hand appeared to function. At first he feared he was paralyzed, but twisting his head, he saw the dead horse had rolled on him. Stunned, Virgil lay with his face half-submerged in water and mud, and wondered if Thorn would finish the job with a bullet to his head.

He heard hoofs splatter mud and water, and he lifted his eyes enough to see three riders heading south down Main Street. He tried to pull his right hand free, but it was pinned under the flank of the horse. He gave up and waited for help. The gunfire would bring men. He could do little until they pulled the damn horse off him.

Harkness was over him then, pulling at his free arm in an effort to drag him from under the dead horse. Others arrived, and together they rolled the horse off him.

'What's all the shooting about?' a miner asked.

'Hey! Over here,' another miner called from the jail, and the crowd moved in that direction. Virgil and Harkness followed.

There on the floor sat Lauter, holding the back of his neck. He looked up at Virgil and Harkness.

'I had the son-of-a-bitch covered.' Holding the top of the desk, Lauter pulled himself to his feet. 'Whoever hit me must have used a two by four.' Gingerly he touched the right side of his face, swollen and bloody. He winced. 'Damn, I think my cheek bone is bust.'

'We need to get after Thorn,' said Virgil, 'before he gets too big a lead.'

'That son-of-a-bitch won't get away.' Lauter pushed through the crowd to the street. 'I'm deputizing a posse. Who's coming with us?'

The crowd, mostly miners, shook their heads or remained silent. They had jobs, and pursuing a whore wasn't a high priority. Just when Virgil thought they would find no more help, a man emerged out of the crowd.

'I'm with you,' he said.

His left arm hung in a sling and a bandage covered his left cheek.

'You up for this, Gunderson?' asked Lauter.

'Come on,' Gunderson said, 'before they put more distance between us.'

Fifteen minutes later, Virgil and the others were on fresh mounts and headed south.

Just before dawn, they stopped at a small stream and dismounted while the horses drank. Virgil said, 'You know this country, Mr Harkness. Can we catch them?'

Harkness removed his Stetson and ran a sleeve across his forehead.

'They're heading down the mountain. I believe Los Angeles is their destination. Plenty of depots on the way where they can get fresh mounts.' He slapped the Stetson back on his head. 'Yet they got a woman with him, and they got no more than half an hour lead on us.'

'But will we catch them?' Virgil asked.

'I'd say somewhere beyond Mono Lake.' Harkness looked at the three men and spit. 'Tomorrow about sundown. The next morning for sure.'

'Is there more than one route they can take?'

'The stage trail is the only way out, except over the mountains. No man in his right mind, especially a man burdened with a woman, would try that. The passes are still full of snow. That would be suicide.'

Gunderson Lott scooped water in his hands and applied it to the back of his neck and his face.

'We're following three horses,' he said.

'Goddamn, I bet that's the bastard who hit me,' Lauter said. 'Wonder who it is?'

With surprising agility, Gunderson threw the reins over the horse's neck and swung into the saddle. The sling that held his arm appeared to bother him little if at all.

'After Thorn is dead, the whore is mine.' He cast his eyes on Virgil.

Virgil mounted and faced Gunderson. 'Such talk is a foolish waste of time until we have them.' With a kick, he spurred his horse across the stream. The others followed.

12

First light was little more than a thin line caressing the top of the mountains, but the ground remained a black carpet. Coming to a stream, Raven called a halt to water the horses, and Josh took this opportunity to remove a package from his saddle bags, handing it to the girl.

'Riding clothes,' he said.

He took the Shakespeare volume from her, which she had clutched since leaving Bodie. He believed that by now she would have dropped it or thrown it away. It was thick and heavy. He thought briefly of leaving it here, but it meant too much to her. He slipped it in the saddle-bag.

The hills were bare except for the new grass, and the girl had no private place in which to change. Josh and Raven turned their backs and watched the horses. He heard the rustling of her dress as she slid it over her head and, moments later, she stood before him dressed in boy's pants and a plaid shirt that she tied in a knot at her waist. She left the dress on the ground.

'I've been in it for days,' she said. 'It smells of confinement. I never want to see it again.'

They each chewed a piece of beef jerky and drank from the stream. Once they mounted, Josh rode next to the girl, afraid her stamina might be her undoing, but she rode as one accustomed to the saddle. To this point, she had proven far more adaptable than he anticipated.

They stopped at noon, and as the horses drank, Raven looked back up the mountain from which they had descended. Josh followed his gaze. Far up the grassy slope, perhaps a mile or more, a cloud of dust swirled in the breeze.

'How many?' he asked.

Raven held up four fingers.

The girl kneeled at the stream, scooping up water with her hands. She stood, wiping her chin.

'You would make better time without me. I can ride alone from here.'

Ignoring her suggestion, Josh lifted her into the saddle.

'Mr Raven and Sammy Chung have provided us with a plan of escape.' Josh mounted his own horse. 'We just need to stay ahead a while longer.'

They talked little as they rode, saving their strength for the daunting task ahead. Already they could see across the valley where the Sierras rose like an impregnable fortress of jagged peaks. Forests covered the slopes, and high drifts blocked the passes. However, the spring thaw was fast melting the pack, and streams cascaded down the mountains. From so far away, they appeared little more than white ribbons against dark rock.

Within the hour, they came over a ridge and saw before them massive Mono Lake, the Dead Sea of the West, eighteen miles in length, twelve in width. Although Josh had heard many stories about this fabled lake, this was the first time he had seen it. Its sheer size was impressive.

To the east, the ground leveled out, and the lake disappeared into a rising mist. To the west, the water crowded right up against the Sierras. Dead tree husks stood upright in the water like palace guards. Huge boulders, many larger than the largest building in Bodie, crowded the shore. Two islands sat in the middle of this great lake, and on both, thousands of birds congregated. Thousands of others floated in the water.

Like the tracings of an artist, a thin white line followed the edge of the lake, and Josh was about to ask Raven to explain the strange phenomenon when the man said, 'They are white worms. Every year around this time, they gather there in vast piles. When my people hold their celebrations in two weeks, we gorge ourselves on them.'

'Worms?' said Josh.

'They are a delicacy,' said Raven. 'Perhaps if you are ever back this way, you will try them.' He glanced over his shoulder at Josh and the girl. 'A singular accomplishment if you do.'

'And why is that?' asked Josh.

A hint of a smile cracked his lips. 'No white man has ever been brave enough to try.'

'How do you prepare them?' Rosa May said.

'We dry them in the sun and mix them with acorns, berries and grass seeds. We bake it into a bread called cuchaba.'

'I think I would like to try that,' Rosa May said. 'Perhaps, as you said, if one day we return.'

By mid-morning, weaving their way through sparse timber and fallen rocks, they approached the very edge of the lake, and Josh saw that this white line was in actuality a continuous mass of worms, fat piles measuring close to two feet in height by three in thickness.

As if reading his mind, Raven looked back, pointed to the worms and made a shoveling motion toward his mouth. Raven laughed and faced the trail again.

'What did he mean by that?' the girl asked.

'I think he wants to know if we would like breakfast.'

Her face lit up with a smile, the first since they had fled Bodie. 'Mr Raven has a sense of humor. I like that.'

Before noon they entered the town of Lee Vining. Originally it was little more than a way station for the stage line, a one-room building and corrals, but the mining companies decided to build a narrow gage railroad from Mono Lake to Bodie. Train crews had begun to haul in material and store it in the town, which had grown to half a dozen buildings, including a tent saloon.

They stopped long enough to trade in their mounts and buy new ones from the station master. Josh glanced back at Mono Lake where he spotted four riders on the northern shore spurring their mounts.

He tightened his cinch and did the same for the girl. Quickly he lifted her into the saddle. She sprang up with a renewed vigor. The short rest had revitalized her.

'How close are they?' she asked.

'Half an hour.' Josh threw his leg over the saddle.

'Less,' said Raven.

They rode south from Lee Vining, a flat stretch heavy with new grass, the ground wet and marshy, slowing their progress. All the time, Josh kept glancing over his shoulders to see if their pursuers had gained.

Soon they left the grasslands and entered the trees. The country became rocky as well as thickly forested, but Raven led them along a clearly defined path where twin ruts created by stages and wagons had cut a trail.

Before dusk, Raven turned west toward the mountains. They began to climb. The girl slumped in the saddle, and Josh rode close, taking the reins and guiding her mount so she only had to cling to the saddle horn.

'We need to stop soon, Mr Raven,' Josh said. 'Miss Whitefield is at the end of her rope. We all are.'

Raven pointed to a grove of trees a mile further. 'The

trees will give us cover.'

'Can you hang on till then?' Josh asked.

The girl flashed a weak smile and nodded.

By the time they entered the pines, night encased the grove in deep shadows. They found a spot near the edge of trees. Josh jumped out of the saddle and lifted Rosa May down. She leaned into him, and he sat her against a tree. The wind had picked up, and a chill settled over the night. The girl shivered. Josh removed two coats from the saddle pockets, throwing one around her shoulders. He slipped into the other.

'No fire,' Raven said.

While Raven tethered the horses, Josh took his Winchester and propped himself between two large pines where the fallen needles provided a soft bed. The girl dropped beside him. Down the slope, perhaps a mile or more, a campfire came to life, a single beacon in the dark night. At the same time, rising over the eastern mountains, the moon, three quarters full, made its appearance, bathing the mountain and valley below in soft light.

'Do they know we are here?' Rosa May asked.

'We have made no effort to conceal our tracks.'

'Will they come after us tonight?'

'I will keep guard until midnight,' said Josh. 'Mr Raven will then take my place.'

Raven, who had tethered the horses, acknowledged the plan by lying down near his own mount and covering himself with a blanket.

'They closed the distance,' said the girl.

'That is to be expected. We just need to keep ahead for a few hours in the morning.'

'What will we do then?' she asked.

'Once we are free of these mountains, we can make our way to Los Angeles.'

'And then?'

'I have yet to give that much thought. Does it matter?'

She picked up a handful of pine needles and allowed them to shift through her fingers.

'I have seldom given the future much thought. I came to believe I would live in Bodie until I died. There or some place like Bodie.'

'The world is open to us,' said Josh. 'We can go anywhere we want.'

'We?'

He looked down the slope. Even from that distance, he saw the four men gathered around the blaze.

'Why did you take me from that jail?' she asked. 'I am no innocent. I killed that man Smith. I would have killed Gunderson Lott if I had been a better shot.'

'Those men had no right to do what they did.'

Her dark eyes blended with the night, but the moon exposed her pained expression. He said, 'I do not believe you were in control of yourself after those men attacked you. Holding you responsible would be like holding a baby responsible because it cries.'

'You make a convincing case, a lawyer's case,' she said.

He said, 'Then consider this – if you were a man and Smith and Ash and Gunderson Lott attacked you, what do you think the jury would have said? If you were a man, the jury would have said "not guilty", and that assumes it ever came to trial.'

'You believe they convicted me because I am a woman?' she said.

Josh shifted his weight to watch the men in the clearing below. When Rosa May spoke again, her voice said she was puzzled.

'You wanted me. After you came to my cell that second time, I saw it in your eyes. I recognize that look in men's eyes.'

Softly he said, 'I wanted you from the first day I saw you.'

'You never came to me. You could have done. I am a two dollar whore.'

'I had no interest in that.'

'You had no interest in a whore,' she said.

Anger flashed across her face, and she started to rise, but he reached out and took her arm.

'Let me explain. If you want to get angry with me afterward, fine.'

She remained seated, but her face had turned hard and unyielding. He said, 'Do not misunderstand me. I am a man with needs, and sometimes on lonely nights those needs drive me half-crazy. But I wanted a woman who was with me for the long haul, a woman I could depend on and who could depend on me. I wanted more.'

Once again she lost herself deep in thought. Josh returned his attention to the men in the valley. Their fire was dying, and the guard tossed more wood on the coals. The fire blazed to life.

Rosa May stood and looked down at him, then walked away. She returned a moment later, a blanket wrapped across her shoulders. She sat, and leaning into him, enfolded the blanket around them both. He slipped his arm around her. She came willingly, and he kissed the top of her head. He wanted to do more, but such action would endanger them all. After a while, her steady breathing told him she slept.

At midnight Raven took up a position ten feet away, his attention focused solely on the valley below. Josh laid his rifle aside and slid to the ground. He pulled the blanket tighter around himself and the girl. She awoke, moving against him, and his mouth found hers. They kissed slowly, their warm breaths mixing with the cool air.

They lay huddled together, their bodies warming each

other. After only a few minutes, Josh heard her steady breathing. Only then did he close his eyes.

13

Before the sun dropped behind the Sierras, Gunderson spotted the tracks heading up the mountain.

'By God! They have left the trail. They head up to the lakes!' He laughed aloud. 'They have ridden themselves into a trap. There is no way out.'

'You know this area then?' asked Virgil.

'Twice my father sent me up here with crews to search for the signs of gold. I know every inch of ground around these lakes,' said Gunderson.

'Desperate situations make desperate men, and a desperate man is capable of many things,' said Virgil. 'Are you sure Thorn is trapped?'

Gunderson studied the mountains, jagged and full of snow. 'Maybe if he was alone, he could save himself by going deeper into the mountains, but not with the whore. No woman could cross those peaks on foot.'

Harkness dismounted. 'We camp here.'

Virgil said, 'How far ahead are they, Mr Lott?'

Gunderson ran his fingers over his bandaged face as he considered the question. 'Half an hour. Possibly less.'

'Did you hear that, Mr Harkness? Half an hour. That is all the lead they have on us.'

'The horses are on their last legs,' Harkness said. 'So are

we.' A few thin clouds had turned brilliant red with the last rays of the sun, but the ground itself was dark with night. 'In this light, we could walk into an ambush. I ain't looking to get shot up. No, sir, Mr Perry. We camp here. In the morning, we'll be fresh for the chase.'

Lauter grunted his assent and slid out of the saddle. 'We got 'em, and they ain't going nowhere. I need some frijoles and a good night's sleep.'

Virgil was bone-weary from so many continuous hours in the saddle, yet his elation was almost too much to bear. Yet he saw the sense in Harkness' proposal. To proceed any further in this light could end in disaster.

They made camp, finding enough loose timber and grass to make a fire. They warmed beans in a skillet and ate. Afterward, Lauter dragged a bottle from his coat pocket. Virgil said, 'Put that away, Mr Lauter. You'll need all your faculties for tomorrow.'

With a sneer, Lauter jerked the cork free and raised the bottle in a mock toast. Before he could drink, Harkness said, 'Mr Perry is right. Put the bottle away.'

'You trying to tell me what to do, too, Bib?' Lauter said.

'You take one drink of that, and you won't have to piss to get it out of your system,' Harkness said.

Lauter twisted his lips into a snarl. With the palm of his hand, he stuffed the cork in the bottle.

'You're as much a sky pilot as Thorn.'

He rolled up in his blanket and turned his back to the fire.

Virgil stood guard first. The others threw blankets around themselves and stretched out on the ground. The fire was dying. Virgil piled more wood on the embers. The dry wood caught and flared. Turning away from the blaze, he cast his gaze up the dark mountain. A three-quarter moon had risen behind him, and he could see all the way to the grove of trees less than a mile away. Surely Thorn could see the fire, and he must understand his hours were numbered, that tomorrow would bring his death.

Near midnight, Virgil woke Harkness. Virgil lay down, rolling up in a blanket. Soon he was warm and comfortable, but he had trouble sleeping. Thorn was too close.

An hour before dawn he came fully alert. He sat up and faced Lauter who had taken over guard duty. Virgil extended his hands over the fire to warm them. Immediately, he smelled the whiskey.

'You have been drinking, sir,' he said.

'Bottle had a crack in it. I tossed it away.'

'You are a liar, sir,' Virgil said.

Lauter held a rifle across his lap and shifted the weapon.

Virgil said, 'I may not be as fast as Mr Harkness, but I am quite proficient with a pistol.'

By this time, the other two men were awake, and Harkness came and stood over Lauter.

'What's the trouble?' he asked.

'The son-of-a-bitch called me a liar,' said Lauter.

Harkness spit. 'Sounds like he's got you pegged.'

Lauter sniffled like he had a cold. Using the stock of the rifle, he pushed himself to his feet.

As the sun lit the top of the eastern mountains with a thin ribbon of orange, they saddled their horses and broke camp. Once they mounted, Harkness said, 'We better watch our step. In this light, we might stumble on them unexpectedly.'

They spread out along the slope. Each man carried a rifle except for Gunderson, who kept his hand close to his pistol.

They entered the trees and found the dry camp. The sun had risen above the top of the White Mountains, providing enough light to see the ground and the footprints in the soft earth.

'The third member of their group wears soft boots,'

Gunderson said.

'What does that mean?' asked Virgil.

'He's got an Indian with him. A Paiute,' said Gunderson.

'A guide,' said Virgil.

'Damn!' said Lauter. 'He'll get away. And that damn whore will get away, too.'

Gunderson knotted his brow. 'Mammoth Lakes are a dead end, I tell you. They can't ride their horses over these mountains. On foot, we'll catch them for sure.'

'Then why did they come this way?' asked Harkness. 'This Paiute must know what's up there, same as you.'

'I have no idea . . .' Gunderson began, and then his face lit with understanding. 'They're headed for Granite Pass. It's the only way out. The pass is narrow and full of snow. Their horses will be useless there. They knew if they held to the stage route, we would have caught them by now. They came this way because they plan to try the pass.' He pointed to a large jagged piece of mountain that dominated the land-scape. It stood straight, and the ridges bent one on top of the other so that from below it appeared like a giant hand pointing toward heaven.

'There's a path, no more than a deer trail really,' said Gunderson. 'It runs along the base of the mountain and all the way up to the pass itself. No horse could traverse it, but a man on foot can cut off three or four hard miles by taking it.'

'You saying we could beat them to the pass?' asked Harkness.

'If they saw us, they might double back,' said Gunderson.

Virgil saw the solution immediately. 'Mr Lott and I will travel the deer trail. Mr Harkness and Mr Lauter – you two keep to their trail. That way we can catch them between us.'

'If they double back, me and Bib will handle them.' Lauter patted his Winchester.

Harkness and Lauter rode on up the trail. Gunderson and Virgil broke off across an open meadow. When they reached the base of the deer trail, they dismounted and hobbled their horses. Virgil went to help Gunderson who was struggling with his one good hand. As he slipped the loop over the legs of the animal, Virgil glanced up the trail, which appeared steep and difficult.

'Are you up for this, Mr Lott?' Virgil asked.

Without replying, Gunderson started up the trail. Virgil followed. He wished he had taken the lead, but the trail was too narrow and the slope too severe for him to pass. A misstep and a man would take a nasty tumble. A thousand yards further, the slope became even sharper, and they clung to a path no more than a foot in width. Several times they hit wet spots, making the footing even more treacherous. With his left arm tied securely against his body, Gunderson had a difficult time keeping his balance, and once his right foot slid off into space. Virgil steadied him.

A breeze blew down from the passes, bringing with it the smell of snow. Virgil pulled his coat tighter, buttoning it all the way to his neck. Every time he lifted his eyes to what lay ahead, he saw the white mass of snow. He had never seen so much snow in his life. Fearing the sheer mass of it, he wanted to turn back, but he held a steady course. They would soon have Thorn and his companions in a pincer, cut off from the pass and cut off from retreat. Virgil put aside his fear and pushed on.

A half mile further up the trail, they came to snow that clung to the slopes, and even the path itself was covered in a thin crust. Their progress slowed to little more than a shuffle.

'This is impossible,' said Virgil. 'We should turn back.'

Gunderson waved off the complaint. He was breathing heavily.

129

Virgil, too, felt the effects of the altitude. He sucked air through his mouth, and his chest burned. A pain spread from his back to his side.

After more than an hour on the path, Virgil was sure that Thorn and his companions had made Granite Pass ahead of them. He said so to Gunderson.

Gunderson pointed to an open space ahead. There the trees abruptly ended, and beyond them, stood a meadow, the snow smooth and unmarked.

'Almost there.' Each word sounded forced and painful.

The deer trail continued up to the snow-covered meadow, but the slope increased at an even greater angle. Twenty-five or thirty feet below, rocks raised their rounded tops out of the snow like threatening fists. His feet sliding in the mud, Gunderson leaned into the mountain to keep his balance.

The first rider emerged out of trees, a dark man dressed in a heavy coat and sporting a wide brim Stetson with a pointed crown. Next came the girl and then Thorn, all riding single file. Virgil felt his heart beat faster. Quickly he worked the lever of his Winchester.

Gunderson drew his .44, cocking and firing in one continuous movement. The blast rocked him back on his heels, and his feet went out from under him. Flailing with his one good arm, Gunderson struck Virgil a glancing blow, knocking the Winchester from his grasp. Virgil threw himself against the mountain, his fingers digging into crevices as his feet threatened to slip off the path.

Gunderson fell. Screaming, he bounced off the slope before he crashed into the rocks below.

Virgil found solid footing, steadied himself, and reached for his pistol.

14

They saddled their horses in the dark and broke camp. They were a mile further up the mountain before first light caressed an eastern peak. Through a break in the trees, Raven pointed to the monolith where white, wispy clouds curled around the top like a crown.

'Granite Pass lies there,' Raven said. 'We still have a hard ride ahead of us.'

For over an hour, they followed a stream that tumbled from above. Here, as light streaked the horizon, Josh stood in the saddle and searched the area behind them, but the dark trees and rocky ground hid their pursuers.

Up until this point, Josh had considered his death a distant possibility. Now, nearing the end of the trail, he saw it as more immediate. He held no romantic illusions about death. He pictured himself lying in the snow, his blood staining the white landscape. For the past year, his life had appeared so full of options, so full of possibilities. Now, as their trail narrowed toward Granite Pass, his options had come down to this one moment.

He pressed his elbow into his side, feeling for the Bible in his coat pocket, but it was not there. He had left it on the desk in his office. Its absence should have alarmed him. He had carried that book for over ten years. But when he remembered all the good people of Bodie calling for the death of the girl, he discovered his anger was greater than his need.

He recalled the verse from Psalm 23: "Yea, though I walk through the valley of the shadow of death, I will fear no evil." Even those words, which ordinarily proved so reassuring, failed to stem his anger.

As if sensing trouble, he removed the Winchester from the rifle boot, cradling the weapon in his arms. Rosa May glanced in his direction.

'A precaution,' he said.

They rode for another hour, weaving their way around trees and boulders but always climbing and always heading toward the monstrous black rock beyond which lay freedom and safety.

The sun broke above the eastern mountains, and in an instant their world was full of light. Raven left the protection of the trees and rode into a clearing. The girl followed, her horse leaping into the snow. Josh spurred up beside her to give her help if she needed it.

The shot came from their left, loud in the crisp air. Josh leapt from his horse, crashing into Rosa May, and together they tumbled into the packed snow. Rising to his knees, Josh worked the lever of his Winchester and brought the rifle to his shoulder. He saw Gunderson topple off into space, striking the slope before he disappeared from view.

On the side of the mountain, another man clung to the rock ledge with one hand, his other clawing at his pistol. Josh shouted, 'Hold it right there, Mr Perry!'

Virgil eyed the Winchester lined up on his chest.

Josh squeezed the trigger until the slack was gone. Only a little more pressure would send Virgil crashing after Gunderson.

Josh said, 'Drop your pistol.'

'If I do that, you will kill me,' Virgil said.

'I could kill you now, if I wished,' said Josh.

Raven looked down from the saddle, his face passive, uninterested. 'Kill him. One less to worry about.'

'I am no deliberate killer,' Josh said.

Virgil took only a moment to consider that fact before he tossed away his .44.

'I trust you have no other weapons, Mr Perry,' said Josh.

'I have a knife, but I do not think it will reach from here.'

Josh stepped to the edge of the ravine. Below him lay Gunderson, his body twisted on the rocks, his eyes closed. A piece of blood-spattered bone jutted through one pants leg. His chest rose and fell in an irregular pattern. Josh felt no pity for the bastard, not after what he had done to Rosa May.

Holding out his hand, Josh helped Rosa May to her feet.

From the saddle, Raven said, 'We must be on our way.' Throwing one leg over the horse, he dismounted. He cradled a Sharp's rifle and headed off toward the pass. His mount stood with her head lowered, her breath a frosty mist.

Josh said to Rosa May, 'Come, let us follow Mr Raven.'

She cast a quick glance back at the trail.

'Do not worry what lies behind,' Josh told her. 'Concentrate on what lies ahead.'

For such a big man, Raven moved like a deer even at this altitude, over 9,000 feet, nimble and fast, his boots kicking up ice and snow with each step. Holding on to Rosa May, Josh breathed through his mouth, trying to draw oxygen deep into his lungs, his chest burning with the effort. His legs ached. Rosa May fared no better. When he looked into her face, he saw her exhaustion.

Josh wanted to risk a look back, but he had warned the girl against such thoughts, and he would not give in to that temptation. They entered the pass, sheer walls rising on both sides as the trail led upward. Josh stumbled and went down on one knee. With the girl pulling at his arm, he got to his feet. Ignoring his own advice, he glanced back.

Lauter and a much smaller man emerged from the trees, their horses kicking up snow. They were 200 yards away, but moving at their speed, they would catch Josh and the girl within minutes.

Fifteen feet ahead lay a large rock that had fallen from the cliffs and blocked the trail. No horse could pass. However, an opening existed, one large enough to allow men walking single file. If they could reach that opening, Josh could hold them off. As it was, they were exposed and vulnerable.

The first bullet shattered splinters from the boulder ahead. The second sprayed snow to their left. By that time Raven had passed to the other side. Josh pushed Rosa May ahead. Working the lever of his Winchester, he turned, dropped to one knee and snapped off a shot, the bark echoing off the walls. He followed that with five others, one blast coming so quickly on top of the other that he never took time to aim. The shots produced an immediate effect. The horsemen leapt from their saddles and dove for the ground. Taking his time, Josh fired once more and snow exploded next to Lauter's head. Lauter screamed and rolled away.

Spinning, Josh ran between the boulder and the cliff, the fit so tight that his broad shoulders scraped hard rock. He ducked down behind the boulder as another bullet ricocheted past.

Raven popped his head over the top and fired the Sharp's, the boom as loud as a canon. As he dropped back, another explosion burst from further up the trail, and a bullet whined over their heads.

Both Josh and the girl looked to see from whom this new attack came. Raven never lifted his head as he broke open the breech of his weapon, expelled the used shell and slipped in a live round.

'My cousin, Snow Eagle. Now we best go while we have our pursuers at a disadvantage.'

They ran in a crouch. The trail rose for perhaps fifty feet where Raven's cousin glued himself to the side of the canyon and waved for them to hurry.

Raven arrived first and waited until Josh and Rosa May reached them. Together the two Paiutes half-carried Rosa May to the horses. They lifted her into a saddle.

Snow Eagle was an old man, well past sixty, his face weathered and full of liver spots. The four horses were skittish and would have run had he not hobbled them. The old man tossed the reins first to Josh and then to Raven. Rather than untie the hobbles, he drew his knife and sliced the ropes one after another. Snow Eagle spoke to Raven in his own language, and he showed gaps between his brown-stained teeth. With the agility of a man many years his junior, he leapt aboard his mount.

They set off for a grove of trees a hundred yards away. Snow Eagle took the point followed by Rosa May and Josh. Raven brought up the rear. As they started up the slope, Rosa May fought for control of her mount as it shied away and reared back. Josh rode up beside her. Gripping the bridle, he forced the animal forward. Just as they entered the trees, a bullet cut through the pine needles above them. Two more shots followed in quick succession.

15

Virgil lowered himself over the trail and fought for hand and toe holds. Gunderson was an arrogant fool, but for two days they had ridden the trail as companions. Virgil felt obligated to help the injured man.

Halfway down, he heard the bark of rifles. The vibrations sent small patches of snow cascading from above, and he had a sudden fear that the shots might bring down a whole mountain of snow. If that happened, he would rest there for eternity, for he was certain that neither Lauter nor Harkness would take the time to dig him free.

He reached Gunderson and knelt beside him as another burst of gunfire erupted, but the sounds were muted by distance and terrain. He wondered if that signaled the end of Thorn and the girl, and he experienced an odd sensation of regret. He never believed he could feel this way, not after pursuing the man for three years, not after following him into this godforsaken country of dark mountains and numbing cold. Yet Thorn had held Virgil's life in his hands. With one squeeze of the trigger, he could have sent him straight to hell.

Gunderson moaned, ending Virgil's musings. The boy was not exactly conscious, but his eyes fluttered. Bone of the left shin had torn its way through flesh and pants, spraying dark blood against the white snow. Gently Virgil ran his hands along the leg, bent at an awkward angle. The mere touch elicited a groan from Gunderson, and Virgil ceased his probing.

For the moment he could do little for the boy. He searched for his rifle and pistol. He found them half buried in the damp snow, and he brushed them clean and checked the barrels to make sure they were unplugged. Satisfied, he returned to Gunderson.

'Mr Perry,' Harkness shouted from the ridge above. 'Are you all right, sir?'

Lauter stood beside Harkness. Virgil said, 'I am fine, but we have a problem.'

Lauter said, 'They had horses waiting. Thorn got away. But I put one in the girl. I know I did.'

Harkness glanced at him out of the corner of his eye, his expression one of doubt.

'Is that so, Mr Harkness?' Virgil asked.

Harkness shrugged. 'They were a hundred yards away heading into a grove of trees. Their mounts were skittish.'

'I put one in her, I tell you.' Lauter appeared angry, the veins on his neck standing rigid.

Harkness turned his cold gaze on the big man. 'Maybe you did, maybe you didn't. Leave it at that.' Using his rifle, he pointed to Virgil and Gunderson. 'Now let's get down there and see if we can help Mr Lott.'

The two men circled around through the woods and half an hour later found a trail into the ravine. As they gathered around Gunderson, Lauter said, 'Damn, Gun! You poor bastard.' Lauter looked up at the face of the cliff and whistled through his teeth. 'He's lucky to be alive.'

Harkness spit. 'Maybe not so lucky. With that leg, he'll never walk again. Add that to what the girl did to his shoulder and face – maybe he'd be better off if the fall had finished the job.'

'But the fall did not kill him,' said Virgil. 'Now we must find a way to get him out of here.'

'He is a dead man, Mr Perry,' said Harkness. 'I don't aim to waste my time on a dead man. Hell, it would take a good week, maybe more, just to get him to Lee Vining. That's assuming he'd live that long.'

Harkness was probably right. The boy would probably die along the trail. As a man, Gunderson was hardly worth the effort, yet Virgil felt compelled to try.

'I promised you a bonus if we got Thorn,' Virgil said.

'Thorn got away. You'll never catch him now, so I guess I'll just have to give up on that bonus. I'll round up one of the horses and be on my way.'

'You and Mr Lauter can split the bonus if you help me get Mr Lott back to Lee Vining,' Virgil said.

Harkness and Lauter cast glances at each other. 'And if he dies?' asked Harkness.

'The bonus is still yours.'

16

Once among the trees, they dropped below a ridge. Behind them, their pursuers kept firing, the sounds of their rifles echoing off the canyon walls, but their bullets flew through the trees and over their heads. Josh risked a look back at Rosa May, who gripped the saddle horn with both hands. She flashed a reassuring smile.

They rode for almost twenty minutes, working their way through trees and around rocks before they came to a stream that cascaded from the mountain high above. As they were about to cross, Rosa May spoke one word.

'Wait. . . .' Her voice was weak as if she were very tired.

Josh leapt to the ground and lifted her out of the saddle. She leaned into him, and without warning, sat down in the snow.

She laid her head against his leg.

'If I could just sleep ' She went limp, and he swept her up in his arms.

Snow Eagle turned his horse and rode back. Josh looked to Raven.

'My friend will see if we are followed,' Raven said.

Josh unbuttoned the girl's coat and slipped it off her shoulders. High in her back was a bloody hole as large as the end of his thumb. Dark blood flowed out in a steady stream. He found no exit wound, and his heart sank. Taking the kerchief from his neck, he pressed it against the wound, applying pressure. Removing his belt, he strapped it over her shoulder and around her bosom. He tightened it and spread the coat back over her shoulders.

Minutes passed, and the girl stirred in his arms. At last they heard a horse plowing through the snow, and Snow Eagle emerged from the trees.

The old man spoke a few words, and Raven said, 'No one follows.'

'What can we do?' asked Josh.

'There is a hogan,' Raven said. 'Up the mountain. A hard climb.' He stood, his face reflecting his concern. 'Nevertheless, we must go there.'

Josh mounted. Raven scooped up the girl and passed her to Josh.

The way proved rocky and steep, and the horses fought to carry their loads. Often their footing slipped, and they almost went down, but each time they righted themselves and continued on. They came to the bottom of a high granite wall where time and again they made detours around large boulders that had fallen from above. Then, as they rounded a cliff face, they rode under a natural overhang where the cliff curved inward from the top. The hogan was here, built from trees and brush and protected from falling rocks and heavy snows.

They laid the girl in the dark interior, and Josh sat by her side. Snow Eagle gathered sticks and built a fire. Soon flames cast moving shadows off the walls. A hole at the top allowed the smoke to filter out. Even so, much of it was trapped within the hogan. The warmth was welcome and comforting.

Raven stood over the girl, his dark face almost lost in the shadows. 'I may be able to help, if you allow me.'

'Why would I not?' asked Josh.

'Because of the color of my skin, and the color of hers.'

'That makes no difference now or ever,' said Josh.

Raven squatted beside Rosa May. He opened her coat, and gently separated the torn shirt, removing the makeshift bandage. Leaning in close, he studied the wound. When he had seen enough, he sat back, his legs crossed. He spread the palm of one hand across his chest.

'The bullet lies where the wind of the soul is lodged.'

'Her lungs,' said Josh.

'We can make her comfortable,' said Raven. 'There is little else we can do.'

Josh wrapped her in blankets and used pine needles to make a pillow. When she awoke that evening, her eyes were dull with fever. She coughed, and blood flecked her lips. Josh wiped her mouth, lifted her head and gave her water. Earlier, Snow Eagle left the hogan and returned with a handful of herbs and roots and two rabbits. He boiled all together, making a broth for Rosa May. The three men ate the meat. Once they finished, they tossed the slender bones in a pile that Snow Eagle scooped up and took outside. Beside a tall pine, he covered the bones with leaves and gave thanks to the rabbits for being so kind to provide sustenance.

The broth appeared to give Rosa May some strength. She rolled her dark eyes to Josh and said, 'I'm dying, aren't I?'

Raven said, 'You go soon to that place where we all go.' He laid a reassuring hand on her arm. 'You will meet the Great Spirit, and then you will see that every end is also a beginning.'

He spoke the words softly, and the melodic poetry appeared to bring a sense of peace to the girl.

With a closed fist, Josh struck the ground. 'I should have ambushed them along the trail. I could have delayed them, maybe made them turn back.'

'Do not talk of blame,' Raven said. 'She does not want to hear it. Tell her what she wants to hear.'

He turned his eyes to the girl. 'What have I got to say that matters?'

'We never – even. . . .' Her dark eyes pleaded, and he understood immediately what she was about to say.

'We would have, when you were ready,' he said. 'When you trusted me.'

She closed her eyes and slept.

The sun dropped behind the mountains and darkness descended on the hogan. When the only light was from the fire, she opened her eyes and asked in a hoarse whisper, 'Why did you do it, Josh?'

'I could not help myself,' he said.

She hung on for two days fighting the pain and fever. Josh and Raven did their best to make her comfortable. Except for rare moments of lucidity, she was delirious, mumbling incoherently and thrashing about. During the early morning of the third day, Josh awoke to discover Raven beside her, his massive hand holding hers.

An hour later, Josh wrapped her body in a blanket and tied it across the saddle of one of the horses. Raven said, 'Where do you go?'

'Down the mountain. I'll find a place to bury her, a nice place, one I think she'd like.'

'And after that?'

'Back to Bodie.'

'Revenge makes the heart stronger. I will go with you, if you wish.'

'If you go with me, you will be an outlaw. White men would hunt you down. You have been a good friend. I will not sacrifice you for my needs.'

'Then perhaps we will meet again, if not on this side then perhaps the other where grass is always green and water always flows.'

As Josh rode down the mountain, leading the horse that carried Rosa May, he discovered an amazing fact. He no longer believed in God. At least, not the Christian God. In that way, he had traveled a far journey indeed since he had first entered Bodie a year before. The simple religion of the Paiutes was a great deal more honest and a great deal more practical. Yet he couldn't accept that religion either. Perhaps he would never again believe in any god, certainly not one who allowed a decent girl like Rosa May to suffer such a life.

Reaching the shores of Convict Lake late in the evening, he came across a young prospector whose beard was tangled and whose hands were calloused. Josh borrowed a shovel. He took Rosa May to a meadow and dug a grave where she had a view of the mountains and the lake. Once Josh finished, he removed the Shakespeare volume from his saddle-bags. He laid the book with Rosa May. As Josh shoveled in the dirt, he felt like crying, but he hardened his heart. He would not cry, not now, not until after he had seen to business.

Once he filled the grave, Josh tied two pieces of sticks together and pounded it in the ground. He saw the irony of the marker, but it was the only one people would recognize and not disturb.

'That cross ain't going last long,' said the young prospector. 'Not out here, not in these mountains.'

Josh handed him his shovel. 'I will put up a permanent marker as soon as I can.'

The prospector looked about the meadow and mountains. 'T'aint nobody going to see it out here.'

'I will put it in a place where they'll see it,' Josh said.

He mounted his horse and rode off toward Bodie.

PART III
BACK TO BODIE

'When the warm weather returns to Bodie, the under-taker dusts off his gorgeous death wagon, the grave digger buys a new spade, and the man who carves epi-taphs on imperishable marble lays in a stock of new chisels.'

—quoted in *The Weekly Bodie Standard*,
June 10, 1880

17

A week to the day since Gunderson had taken his fall, they rode into Lee Vining carrying their broken comrade on a litter made of tree branches and rope. He was still alive, but the left leg was streaked with red and swollen to twice its size. They left Gunderson with a doctor who worked for the railroad, his hospital little more than a one room log cabin.

Later, the doctor found the three men at the bar sharing drinks. He was a young man who hid his face behind a thick brown beard.

'Gangrene has set in.'

'Poor bastard.' Lauter sipped his whiskey.

Harkness stared at himself in the mirror behind the bar.

The doctor held up two fingers to the bartender who handed over two bottles of whiskey.

'I need help to take off the leg,' said the doctor.

'I ain't got the stomach for that.' Lauter turned his back and stood shoulder to shoulder with Harkness.

Virgil laid his glass on the bar and followed the doctor. As they exited the saloon, the doctor said, 'Your friends do not appear anxious to help.'

'Not friends,' said Virgil. 'Companions only.'

'And this Gunderson. The man on whom I am to operate. Is he a friend?'

'No more than the other two.'

'Yet you spent a great deal of time and effort to save him.' The doctor uncorked one of the bottles.

'I could not leave a man to die alone in the mountains.'

The young doctor stopped, took a long drink from the bottle and held it out for Virgil.

'I thought the whiskey was for Gunderson,' Virgil said.

'It is.' The doctor tilted his head back, took another drink before lowering the bottle. 'Have you ever cut into anyone's flesh, Mr Perry?'

'I have dug bullets out of men,' Virgil said.

'Have you ever hacked off a man's arm or leg?' The doctor ran a sleeve across his mouth. 'It is an unnatural act, a monstrous act. I won't get drunk, but I must fortify myself. I advise you to do the same.'

'I best not cloud my senses.'

'Suit yourself, Mr Perry.' The doctor slapped the cork back into the bottle.

'Does Gunderson understand what is about to happen?' Virgil asked.

'If I told him, he would fight me. Most men do when they're about to lose an arm or a leg.' The doctor held out his right hand, and seeing it was steady, he smiled. 'We will get him drunk, and then cut away. If he survives and wants to kill himself, that's his business. We will have done our duty.'

When they entered the cabin, Virgil was struck by the putrid smell of decaying flesh. Even with the window open and the cool breeze coming off Mono Lake, the stench was overpowering.

Gunderson was awake, his eyes narrowed with fatigue and pain. The doctor handed him a bottle. 'This will help the pain, Mr Lott. Drink it all. Get good and drunk. It will help you sleep. You need your rest if you are to recover.'

Gunderson looked past the doctor to Virgil. 'You did me

no favor, sir. You should have put a bullet in my head and left me in the mountains.' His voice was a hoarse whisper.

The doctor lifted Gunderson's head, and tilting the bottle, poured the liquor down his throat. At first, Gunderson coughed and spit, but then he swallowed whole mouthfuls. Thirty minutes later and well into the second bottle, he passed out.

The doctor opened a drawer and took out different sized knives, a hacksaw and an instrument that resembled a meat cleaver. He laid them side by side, the metal gleaming in the dim light of the cabin.

'You hold him down, Mr Perry. Keep him from thrashing. And for your own peace of mind, try not to look too closely. I have seen the strongest of men grow faint under such circumstances.'

After it was over and the doctor tied up the loose skin to seal the stump, he wrapped the leg in a blanket and carried it a hundred yards from the nearest building. He dropped it in a hole that he had dug earlier. With a shovel, he spread quicklime over the blanket and around the edges of the hole.

Standing beside the doctor, Virgil breathed deeply. The fresh air helped to dispel some of his nausea. The doctor had proven right about the obscenity of hacking into a man's flesh. The sight had turned his stomach far beyond what he thought possible.

As they walked back to the cabin, Virgil asked, 'Will he live?'

'When a man loses an arm or a leg, it is a shock to his system. He was already weak from loss of blood.' He shrugged. 'Tonight and tomorrow will deliver his fate.'

Virgil returned to the saloon where he found Harkness engaged in a card game with four railroad workers. Lauter sat in a corner by himself, bleary-eyed and half-drunk. Virgil strolled to the bar where he ordered a whiskey. Seeing him, Harkness threw his cards into the pile, swept his few coins from the table. The man wore a sour expression, and Virgil guessed the little man had run into a streak of bad luck. He came to stand beside Virgil.

'You owe me and Lauter money.'

'And I intend to pay.' Virgil lifted the glass and downed the drink. The cheap whiskey scalded his throat, but the pain reminded him that he was alive. 'The nearest bank is in Bodie.'

'Then that is my destination, also,' Harkness said.

The next morning on their way out of Lee Vining, Virgil stopped at the doctor's cabin. The doctor came out to meet them.

'He survived the night,' said the doctor.

'Gun is a strong man,' Lauter said.

'Less than a man now.' Harkness spit, the white globule slapping the dark earth. 'Let's ride. I am sick of this place.'

Once they left the shores of Mono Lake, the climb was steep, which made for slow going. That night they camped beside a stream, still eight miles from Bodie. Before first light, clouds moved over the Sierras, and rain began to fall. The men donned their slickers, but soon the ground was too wet to offer comfort. They broke camp, mounted their steads and rode in the dark, the rain beating their backs. Tired and sleepy, they entered Bodie.

Lauter went off to the marshal's office where he said he would sleep in one of the bunks in the cells. Virgil and Harkness continued on to the Bodie Feed and Livery where they left their mounts in charge of the stable boy.

'Guess I'll get a room at the Bodie Hotel.' Harkness said. 'What about you, Mr Perry?'

'I will see you at the bank at twelve, Mr Harkness. Now if you don't believe I'll be there, you are free to come with me.

I am going to see the Lott family to tell them about Gunderson.'

'Until twelve, Mr Perry,' Harkness said.

As Virgil climbed the stairs to the Lott house, his bones ached with fatigue. He knocked, and when no one answered, he knocked again. Susan Lott opened the door and peered out.

'Yes?'

The interior was dark, and Virgil wondered if he had awakened the household. He removed his sombrero. 'Miss Lott, my name is Virgil Perry. I need to speak to your father.'

'Let him in,' said a gruff voice behind the girl.

Susan Lott stepped away to allow Virgil to enter.

'You will not move, sir, or I will be forced to shoot,' said the voice.

Virgil located the man standing beside the velvet curtain that lined the living room entrance. He was much thinner than when Virgil had last seen him, but his tall figure was easily recognizable. In his hand he held a .45 pointed at Virgil's belly. His chest was bare, but his left shoulder and side were heavily bandaged. His face was white and bloodless, but his eyes burned with a fire, reminding Virgil that Marshal Grey was the most dangerous man he had ever faced.

Grey said, 'You are a friend of Bib Harkness.'

'He was my traveling companion, but I have no fondness for the man,' said Virgil. 'I knew nothing of Harkness' intentions before I came to Bodie. I hired him as a guide.'

'Then why are you here?'

'I came to see Mr Lott about his son,' said Virgil.

A body moved from behind Grey into the light. 'Gunderson? What about Gunderson?' Then, fearing the worst, he asked, 'Is he alive?'

'He was when I left yesterday morning.' Virgil glanced at the girl, afraid to speak in her presence since she was, after all, a woman of refinement. 'Perhaps we should speak in private, Mr Lott.'

The girl understood.

'I think Mother needs me,' she said and climbed the stairs to the dark landing. Virgil admired her intuitive sense of decorum.

Mr Lott said, 'When Gunderson didn't return, I feared the worst.'

'Your son sustained a bad fall.' Virgil explained the extent of the injury and the details concerning the manner in which it happened. 'I am sorry to be the bearer of such bad news. In the end, it was no one's fault. An accident, a false step, a slip.'

'We must go to him,' Mr Lott said and rushed up the stairs after his daughter, leaving Grey and Virgil alone in the antechamber.

Grey still held the pistol, but it hung at his side. The two men stared at one another. Virgil had exhausted his words, and with a nod, he turned to go. Grey said, 'What happened to Thorn?'

'Thorn and the woman made it through Granite Pass ahead of us. That is all I know.'

Grey stuck the pistol in his belt. 'I understand you came to kill Thorn.'

'Thorn killed my brother. I intended to extract my revenge.'

'You plan to go after him?'

'Thorn had me in the sights of his rifle, but he allowed me to live. I must give that some thought.'

'Did Harkness and Lauter come back with you?'

'Yes.'

'My argument is with them.' Grey's fingers touched the pistol in his waistband. 'When trouble comes, can I count on you to stay out of it?'

151

'I owe them money for helping me with Gunderson. Otherwise, I want nothing to do with either man.'

Virgil walked to the Bodie Hotel where he rented a room. Once alone in his bed, he discovered that, despite his exhaustion, he had trouble sleeping. The light from the east streamed through his window, and he lay staring at the ceiling. He wondered what the hell he was going to do with the rest of his life.

At noon he met Harkness and Lauter at the bank where he cashed a draft for $1000 and gave each man $500.

Pocketing the money, Lauter said, 'How 'bout a drink to celebrate?'

Lauter again wore the marshal's badge pinned to his chest. He had buffed the metal to a bright finish.

'Will you join us, Mr Perry?' asked Harkness.

'Our business is concluded.' Virgil crossed the bank floor and exited the building.

Harkness came out behind him and said, 'That's an unfriendly attitude, Mr Perry.'

Virgil turned to face Harkness. 'Are you going to shoot me because I do not wish to drink with you, Mr Harkness?'

Harkness spit. 'This is my town now, Mr Perry, and I don't like being insulted in my town.'

'I have not insulted you yet.' Virgil allowed his wrist to touch the .44 on his hip. 'However, if you need to force the issue, I will oblige.'

Doubt clouded Harkness' eyes. After a moment's hesitation, he gave a crooked smile. 'I have no quarrel with you, Mr Perry. You just paid me good money.' To Lauter he said, 'Let's go get that drink.'

Perry watched as the two walked toward the Emporium, and he allowed himself to breathe easier. If it had come to a shooting, he had no doubt Harkness would have killed him. Harkness was much faster on the draw than he. Only the doubt in Harkness' mind had saved him. The smart thing now was to pack his things and get out of town before the gunman pushed the issue again. Ignoring his own counsel, Virgil followed after Harkness and Lauter.

In the Emporium, he found a table in a corner and ordered a drink. When the waiter brought it, Virgil let it sit on the table untouched. Harkness and Lauter were already at the bar. When Harkness looked in the mirror and noticed Virgil, he raised his glass in a salute. Virgil acknowledged the gesture with a nod, the brim of his sombrero bobbing. He was unsure why he had come, only that he had a feeling, vague though it was, that something was about to happen.

At this time of day, the Emporium was crowded with miners stopping for beer and free eats, but everyone in the room knew of Harkness and his encounter with Grey. As a result, they gave him a wide berth. He and Lauter, their backs to the door, were enjoying their drinks and congratu-lating each other on their recent good fortune. Neither saw Grey push through the swinging doors, the .45 in his right hand.

That movement in the mirror caught Harkness' atten-tion. He dropped his glass and spun around, his hand clawing for his pistol.

The .45 exploded.

Men screamed and dove for cover.

The bullet struck Harkness high in the chest, passing through the little man and shattering a bottle on the bar. Harkness stood upright ten seconds or more as he stared at Grey in glassy-eyed shock. His knees buckled, and his but-tocks slammed into the sawdust-covered floor. Blood poured from his chest, staining the front of his shirt.

The acrid smell of gun smoke filled the room, and the patrons, shocked by what happened, picked themselves off the floor and from under tables. Virgil came to stand beside

Grey. At their feet, Harkness gasped for breath, his body twitching. Disbelief frozen on his face, he toppled sideways, his head bouncing against the brass foot-rail.

Turning on Lauter, Grey pressed the .45 against the belly of the big man. 'Take off that badge.'

Lauter plucked the badge from his vest and dropped it on the bar.

Grey laid his pistol on the bar, the butt toward him. He pinned the badge on himself, all the time keeping his eyes on Lauter, who stood immobile, rooted by fear.

Grey swept up his pistol and raked the barrel across Lauter's face. Lauter stumbled back, his hands gripping the bar for support. The skin along the cheekbone lay open, and blood flowed down Lauter's neck, staining his kerchief and shirt collar. Grey shoved the pistol in his belt.

'Get out of Bodie. Now. Because the next time I see you, I will kill you.'

Lauter pressed a palm against his busted cheek. Blood streamed between his fingers. His eyes darted to Virgil. 'You on his side, too?'

'I believe that the marshal is a righteous judge of character,' said Virgil. 'And you, sir, are a coward and a bully.'

Lauter's eyes were alive with hate.

Grey walked away, pushing through the swinging doors. He was no sooner out of the Emporium than Lauter leapt on the bar, reached behind it and came up with a sawn-off shotgun. With a guttural scream, he cocked both barrels and charged across the room.

18

Josh entered Bodie through King Street, the Chinese section. Once he neared the home of Sammy Chung, he dismounted, tied his mare to a hitching post, and approached from the rear. As if alerted to his presence, Sammy opened the door.

'I told you, my friend, that life is unpredictable. You have returned when you thought you were gone from here forever.'

Once in the living room, Josh said, 'They killed her, Sammy. They hounded her and killed her.'

'Mr Lauter brags that he is responsible.'

'Lauter.' Josh heard the hatred in his own voice. 'Any idea where he is right now?'

'He is in the Emporium, but he is not alone. The assassin Harkness is with him. And the other man, Virgil Perry, is close by.' Sammy wrinkled his brow. 'I have forgotten my manners. You must be very tired, my friend. You need drink and food. Please. . . .'

He called for Mai Lin. She came and stood in the doorway, her head bowed, refusing to look at the two men. Her eyes were red, her cheeks flushed. Sammy ordered her to bring tea, and the girl began to back out of the room.

'Mai Lin,' Josh said.

She stopped, lifting her eyes.

'She was a good person,' he said. 'Far better than most in this town.'

The girl retreated into the dark interior.

'What is your plan, Joshua?' Sammy asked.

Facing him, his jaw tight, the muscles in his neck rigid, Josh said, 'The only plan I have is to administer a little Old Testament justice.'

'Sacrifices will not bring her back.'

'I'm not looking to bring her back, Sammy.' Josh pressed his hand against the .44 that rested on his hip.

'The odds, my friend, are against you.' Sammy smiled. 'Yet who knows what God has in store for us?'

'Are you giving me that old cliché about God working in mysterious ways?' asked Josh.

'It is not a cliché if one believes in God,' said Sammy. 'Do you still believe in God, my friend?'

'My faith had been tested these past weeks,' said Josh. 'I have serious doubts.'

'Doubt is the beginning of wisdom,' said Sammy. 'Without doubt, there would be no fear.'

Josh held out his hand, and Sammy took it in both of his. 'This may truly be the last time we see each other,' Josh said. 'So let me say it's been a privilege knowing you, Sammy. You have made my time in Bodie memorable.'

Once on the street, Josh kept close to the buildings. As he passed people who recognized him, they stepped aside as if he had leprosy. Approaching Main Street and the Emporium, he drew his pistol, cocking it. He held no romantic illusions about a fair fight. He was more than a competent shot, but he was not fast enough to stand up to Harkness or perhaps even Lauter. His only advantage lay in surprise. If he had to, he would ambush them, shoot them down like rabid dogs, outlast them.

From the Emporium came the sound of a muffled shot, but gunfire in Bodie was far too common to pay it any mind. Perhaps that shot had signaled a death, but here life was cheap, especially in the late spring and summer when the town averaged a killing a day. Today that average was likely to go up.

He stopped behind a wagon across from the Emporium, which was curiously silent. Josh feared his presence was known, and behind those swinging doors Lauter, Harkness and Virgil Perry waited for him.

A man pushed out through the swinging doors. He was much thinner than when Josh had last seen him, almost skeletal, and his left arm dangled in a sling, forcing him to walk stiff-backed. A .45 was stuck in his belt, and a star pinned to the sling.

Grey turned and headed south. He was at the end of the boardwalk when another figure charged through the swinging doors.

Lauter.

The big man lifted the double-barrel Remington and planted his feet wide apart, bracing himself.

Josh threw up his pistol and fired.

Lauter jerked half around, and the shotgun exploded.

Grey spun, drawing his pistol as Josh fired a second time. The impact threw Lauter against the wall of the saloon. Josh walked forward, cocking his pistol.

Lauter tried to bring the shotgun to bear. Josh stopped, steadied his arm, and squeezed the trigger. The weapon jumped, and the bullet tore into Lauter's chest.

Lauter opened his mouth like he was about to speak but had forgotten what he wanted to say. His body went slack, the shotgun dropped from his hands, and he slid down the wall until he sat on the walk, his arms at his sides,

Josh stood over the body, smoke drifting from the barrel

of his .44, the smell of cordite mixing with the stench of blood. Grey came to stand beside him.

'So you came back,' he said.

'I guess I got here at the right time.'

'I don't think I'm going to like being indebted to you,' Grey said.

'Would you prefer the alternative?' Josh asked.

'Point taken.'

'Where's Harkness?' asked Josh.

Grey smiled, the first Josh had ever seen from the tall man. 'In hell, I suspect.'

'And Virgil Perry?' asked Josh.

'I'm right here, Mr Thorn,' Virgil said.

Josh turned to face the man who held a .44 less than a foot from his belly, and he realized with sudden, blinding insight that he had no desire to die. He had too many things he wanted to do, too many places to see, too many people to meet. He swallowed back his fear and looked Virgil in the eye. Virgil said, 'Did you come for me, also?'

'Lauter killed the girl. I came for him.' Josh slid his pistol in the holster. 'However, I do believe you and I have unfinished business, Mr Perry.'

Grey tried to step around Josh to put himself between the two men. Virgil said, 'If you have business with either of us, it is after we are finished.'

'After you kill Thorn, you mean,' said Grey. 'I will not allow that, Mr Perry. This is my town, and I do not tolerate cold-blooded killings.'

'Just tell me about my brother.' Virgil lowered his weapon.

Josh was suddenly weak in the legs. In an effort to control his emotions, he took a deep breath. Yet when he spoke, his voice trembled.

'I went looking for your brother because I wanted him to

understand the pain he had caused, not just to me, but to a great many people. I never went with the idea of killing him. He insulted me, I tried to walk away. He drew his pistol and fired twice before I shot him. He gave me no choice.'

'I never raised Ike to be a back shooter.' In a tight, pain-filled voice, Perry said, 'I am sorry about the girl. That was never my intention.'

'I know that, sir,' said Josh.

'Then I believe our business is completed, Mr Thorn.' Virgil pushed back through the double doors.

Later, Josh and Grey sat in the living room of the Lott house. The Lotts, father, mother and daughter, had left earlier for Lee Vining to be with Gunderson.

'The boy may be dead for all I know,' said Grey. 'According to Mr Perry, Gunderson was in pretty bad shape when they left him. The way I understand it, Harkness and Lauter were all for leaving the boy to die in the mountains. Perry paid them a handsome sum to bring him out.'

'Mr Lott must be taking it hard,' said Josh.

'He is a broken man.'

'And Susan?' Josh asked.

'The old man said something about taking Gunderson to San Francisco. I suspect Bodie has seen the last of the Lott family.' Grey shifted his weight, trying to find a comfortable position for his wounded shoulder. 'What about you, Thorn? Will you stay in Bodie?'

'Will you allow me to stay? After all, I caused you much grief. And I did steal a prisoner from you.'

'You stole a prisoner from Lauter, not me,' said Grey. 'I suspect you did this town a favor. It never set right with most people that we were going to hang a woman. It certainly did not set right with me.'

'She did not deserve what they did to her,' Josh said, and the pain returned with a deadening intensity. Time would dull the hurt, but for now, it was very immediate and very deep.

As if embarrassed, Grey looked away.

The next morning, Josh went to the Bodie Funeral Parlor where he ordered a gravestone carved with the name of Rosa May Whitefield. He waited until the stonemason had finished and accompanied the workmen to the graveyard. He watched while they placed it in the ground near the entrance. Bodie would never allow such a marker within the confines of the cemetery, which was for decent folk, not prostitutes or gamblers or other lowlifes. But Josh made sure that it was situated where everyone who entered would see it. He wanted the town to remember.

As the days turned into months, the pain did fade, but every time he passed that marker, he felt a twinge of regret for what might have been.